Samuel Sharpe

The Decree of Canopus in hieroglyphics and greek

Samuel Sharpe

The Decree of Canopus in hieroglyphics and greek

ISBN/EAN: 9783742843265

Manufactured in Europe, USA, Canada, Australia, Japa

Cover: Foto ©Andreas Hilbeck / pixelio.de

Manufactured and distributed by brebook publishing software
(www.brebook.com)

Samuel Sharpe

The Decree of Canopus in hieroglyphics and greek

THE

DECREE OF CANOPUS,

IN

HIEROGLYPHICS AND GREEK,

WITH

TRANSLATIONS,

AND AN EXPLANATION OF THE HIEROGLYPHICAL CHARACTERS.

By SAMUEL SHARPE,

AUTHOR OF "THE HISTORY OF EGYPT."

LONDON:
JOHN RUSSELL SMITH, 36, SOHO SQUARE.
1870.

WORKS BY THE AUTHOR.

EGYPTIAN HIEROGLYPHICS, being an Attempt to Explain their Nature, Origin, and Meaning; with a VOCABULARY.

EGYPTIAN INSCRIPTIONS from the British Museum and other sources; 216 Plates, in Folio.

The EGYPTIAN ANTIQUITIES in the BRITISH MUSEUM described.

The ALABASTER SARCOPHAGUS of Oimenephah I., with Plates by JOSEPH BONOMI.

The TRIPLE MUMMY-CASE of Aroeri-ao, with Plates by JOSEPH BONOMI.

The HISTORY of EGYPT, from the Earliest Times till the Conquest by the Arabs, in A.D. 640. Fourth Edition.

The CHRONOLOGY and GEOGRAPHY of ANCIENT EGYPT, with Plates by JOSEPH BONOMI.

ALEXANDRIAN CHRONOLOGY.

The CHRONOLOGY of the BIBLE.

The HISTORY of the HEBREW NATION and its LITERATURE.

The HEBREW SCRIPTURES TRANSLATED, being a revision of the Authorized English Old Testament.

The NEW TESTAMENT TRANSLATED from Griesbach's Text. Sixth Edition.

CRITICAL NOTES on the Authorized English Version of the New Testament. Second Edition.

HISTORIC NOTES on the Books of the Old and New Testaments. Second Edition.

TEXTS from the HOLY BIBLE, explained by the Help of the Ancient Monuments. Second Edition.

EGYPTIAN MYTHOLOGY and EGYPTIAN CHRISTIANITY, with their Influence on the Opinions of Modern Christendom.

THE DECREE OF CANOPUS.

INTRODUCTION.

THE following Inscription may be called either the Decree of
Canopus, from the city in which the Egyptian priests met when
they published it, or the Tablet of Tanis, from the spot in which
it was found, and the city for which this copy was carved. It
was found in 1866, by Messrs. Lepsius and Weidenbach, of
Berlin, and Messrs. Reinisch and Roesler, of Vienna; and each
party published a copy of it. The following is copied from that
published in Vienna by the latter gentlemen. It contains thirty-
seven lines of hieroglyphical writing, followed by seventy-five
lines of Greek—one the translation from the other. Each inscription is continuous, with no breaks or spaces between the words.
Above the hieroglyphics is a semicircular picture of a pair of
outstretched wings, but without the Sun, from which these wings
usually spring. From the place of the Sun hang two Asps—
one crowned with the crown of Upper Egypt, and the other with
that of Lower Egypt. Between the Asps are the characters for a
Gift and for Life. On each side of the Asps is a sceptre, in a
horizontal position, which the Asps may be supposed to hold.
The stone is limestone, and, though not hard, the inscription on
it is uninjured. The whole, both of the hieroglyphics and the
Greek, is perfect.

It was happily discovered by Dr. Roesler, on publishing this
Decree, that the sadly mutilated fragment of a bilinguar tablet in
Burton's "Excerpta Hieroglyphica," plates 54 and 55, is a copy
of the same Decree. This stone is now in Paris, in the Louvre.
On comparing the very few characters that can be read upon it

with our perfect copy, we are able to learn, first, that the two
Greek inscriptions probably agreed together word for word, but
not line for line; and secondly, that the two hieroglyphical
inscriptions did not agree character for character. Hence, alone,
we might have concluded that the Greek was the original, and
that the hieroglyphics were the translation. And this is what we
have learnt by comparing the Greek and hieroglyphics in the
perfect tablet. The Paris copy was originally wider than that
found at Tanis, but had been divided down its length, probably
in order to make of it two door-steps, or sills, for which, as it is
of hard stone, it was very suitable; and in some such position it
has been very much worn. It had a more ornamental head-piece.
Under the winged Sun are traces of a row of several gods and
goddesses, and probably there was once a figure of the king
sacrificing to them. Beneath are thirty lines of hieroglyphics, and
seventy-three of Greek. The Paris copy has also the remains
of a third version of the Decree, in the Enchorial or common
letters, not given by Burton.

In the following pages the hieroglyphics are divided, with
spaces between the words, and every word is numbered, for the
convenience of referring to it in the Explanation of the hieroglyphics which follows. At the same time, the position of the
characters is so kept that the reader can understand how they
stood with regard to one another in the more crowded original.
The Greek is not given in the square characters of the original,
but in the letters usually employed in printed books. Both the
hieroglyphics and the Greek are divided into their original lines.

In the Explanation of the hieroglyphical words, first is given its
probable meaning; then the force of its characters in Roman
letters; then the Coptic word which those letters seem to represent.
When a word, as is usually the case, is used several times in the
Inscription, reference is made from one place to another. Reference
is also sometimes made to the Author's Vocabulary, at the
end of his volume entitled *Egyptian Hieroglyphics*. The Coptic
words quoted are all taken from Dr. Tattam's *Lexicon Ægyp-
tiacum*.

The two translations are placed face to face, and broken into paragraphs for more convenient comparison. An Alphabet is added, but it is limited to the letters used in our Inscription. Both translations are as literal as possible, in order to show not only how far they agree, but also how far they differ.

This Decree would have given to us the long wished-for key to the knowledge of hieroglyphics, had we not already obtained that knowledge by means of the Rosetta Stone, which was discovered more than half a century earlier. The Rosetta Stone, thanks to Dr. Young and M. Champollion, had given us a knowledge of several words, and the force of a large number of letters, or syllabic characters. With this beginning, aided by the art of decyphering, by the Coptic language, and by the pictures which accompany many of the Egyptian inscriptions, this number has been largely increased. The new acquisitions are, many of them, as certain as the knowledge gained more directly from the translated inscription. Other results are of less certain value; and some of these this new discovery will enable us to reject, while it confirms others with a double certainty.

The language of this tablet differs not a little from that of Rosetta. In that inscription, as it would seem, the hieroglyphics were the original, and the Greek a translation. But in this Decree of Canopus the Greek seems to be the original, and the hieroglyphics the translation. The consequence is, that in the hieroglyphics of this Decree the thoughts are expressed at far greater length— that is, with the help of a far greater number of words—than in the hieroglyphics of the Rosetta Stone. The Egyptian scribe, in his wish to express accurately the meaning of the more exact language, was forced to use a greater number of auxiliary verbs, and of inflections to his verbs, than we meet with on the Rosetta Stone, or is common in other inscriptions. In this way it makes the Coptic language far more necessary to us, and also far more useful. Again, the Egyptian scribe has made use of his priestly knowledge to give the particulars of some of the rites, which are mentioned by the Greek writer in only general terms; and he has given to the king his Egyptian complimentary titles, which are not found in the Greek. He shows the various ranks of the priests and priestesses, and the various degrees of holiness of the temples, or parts of the temples. He gives to the sacred bread its name of Presence-bread, the very name used in the Hebrew law for the bread eaten by the priests in the Temple of Jerusalem. Thus in our translations the hieroglyphic decree is much longer than the Greek. The scribe has been very inexact in the use of the prepositions; but perhaps not more so than the Coptic language allows.

If a student should wish to pursue an independent inquiry, and to decypher the hieroglyphics for himself without the help, and therefore without the possible mistakes, of former inquirers, he should begin with a number of the names of the Egyptian kings. From the most modern of those, the names of the Roman emperors and of the Ptolemies, he may form an alphabet of nearly one hundred characters. The recurrence of the same characters in the various names will be a proof that the right force has been assigned to each.

He may then begin upon this Decree, not using the translation here given, but making one for himself. In doing so, the proposition is to divide the hieroglyphical inscription into various groups of characters for words in such a manner, that the same hieroglyphical words should correspond as nearly as possible with the same Greek words in the various parts of the Decree. So far as this can be done, the Greek words may be supposed to be a translation of the corresponding hieroglyphics. The hieroglyphical words are then to be compared with the words in the Coptic Dictionary. In this way, when the Greek inscription and hieroglyphic inscription are compared, if a hieroglyphical word is in every case found to correspond in the sentence with the same Greek word, and if also, when read by means of the alphabet, it be found to bear in the Coptic language the meaning which its Greek word gives to it, we may then be satisfied that we have learned its real meaning.

By this appeal to the Coptic language, the student will not only confirm the alphabetic force which he gained for the several characters from the kings' names; but he will add to his alphabet many characters which are not there used. He will also learn the syllabic sound of many characters which, as they contain the sound of two consonants, can take no place in an alphabet.

These are the steps which the Author has pursued; but he is well aware that he has not in every place obtained the wished-for certainty. His translation of the single words is in many cases of doubtful value, and, possibly, often wrong. This arises from two causes: first, the hieroglyphics are not an exact, but a free rendering of the Greek Decree; and, secondly, the language of the hieroglyphics is not quite the same as the Coptic of the Dictionary, which was the language of Egypt four centuries after this inscription was made. If the reader takes the trouble to compare this translation with that made by Dr. Lepsius, or that by Drs. Reinisch and Roesler, he will find that it differs from those in the force given to many of those characters which are less certainly understood, because they are not used in the kings' names. It also differs in its division of the continuous sentence into words, and in the meaning of many of the words. But those gentlemen make no appeal to the Coptic language to support their renderings; and hence we are unable to judge upon what their opinions are founded.

This Decree is valuable to us for other reasons besides its help to the study of hieroglyphics. It tells us of a proposal then made by the priests to reform the Egyptian calendar, at least, so far as it was used in fixing the days when the religious feasts were to be celebrated. Ever since the year B.C. 1322, in the reign of Menophra, probably the king better known as Thothmosis II., the Egyptian civil year had consisted of 365 days; and hence, for want of a leap-year, the new-year's day, and the feasts then cele-brated, were always moving one day earlier every four years. This change, which must in every generation have been noticed, had now, by the help of the Alexandrian astronomers, been determined with greater exactness. The new-year's day, the 1st of Thoth, which ought to fall on the 18th of July, when the Dog Star is seen to rise heliacally, had now, in the ninth year of Ptolemy

Euergetes, moved nearly nine months earlier, and fell on the 22nd of October. This is well known from several observations recorded by the Alexandrian astronomers; and quite agrees—at least, as well as observations which depend upon eyesight and the weather can be expected to agree—with the information contained in this Decree, namely, that the Dog Star then rose heliacally on the 1st of Payni. Calculating back from what we are told by Censorinus, our great authority on the Calendar, we should have supposed that was not the case till the next year, the 10th of Euergetes. The very small disagreement shows with what accuracy the heliacal rising of the star could be observed. However, the priests proposed to be no longer guided by this movable civil year in the arrangement of their feast days. How far their proposal was acted on we do not know. The change was not made by civil authority till the reign of Augustus, who first introduced the Julian mode of reckoning into Alexandria, in the year B.C. 25.

This rather intricate subject will be best understood by the help of the following Table, showing the Egyptian Calendar at the various times at which we have occasion to consider it :—

THE EGYPTIAN CALENDAR.

The Dog-star rises on the 18th July; the New-year's Day.

The Months, with their Names showing the Seasons.	The Natural Year of 365¼ days.	The Civil Year of 365 days, at the Era of Menophra; B.C. 1322.	The Civil Year, at the date of the Decree; B.C. 238.		The Civil Year, when Augustus introduced the Leap-year; B.C. 21.	
Pachon, 1st *(of Inundation.)*	17 Aug.	Thoth, first month.	19 July	Payni.	25 July	Mesore.
Payni, 2nd	16 Sept.	Paophi.	18 Aug.	Epiphi.	24 Aug.	Five days.
Epiphi, 3rd	16 Oct.	Athyr.	17 Sept.	Mesore.	29 Aug.	New-year's Day. Thoth.
Mesore, 4th	15 Nov.	Choeac.	17 Oct.	Five days.	28 Sept.	Paophi.
Thoth, 1st *(of Vegetation.)*	15 Dec.	Tybi.	22 Oct.	New-year's Day. Thoth.	28 Oct.	Athyr.
Paophi, 2nd	14 Jan.	Mechir.	21 Nov.	Paophi.	27 Nov.	Choeac.
Athyr, 3rd	13 Feb.	Phamenoth.	21 Dec.	Athyr.	27 Dec.	Tybi.
Choeac, 4th	15 March	Pharmuthi.	20 Jan.	Choeac.	26 Jan.	Mechir.
Tybi, 1st *(of Housing.)*	14 April	Pachon.	19 Feb.	Tybi.	25 Feb.	Phamenoth.
Mechir, 2nd	14 May	Payni.	21 March	Mechir.	27 March	Pharmuthi.
Phamenoth, 3rd	13 June	Epiphi.	20 April	Phamenoth.	26 April	Pachon.
Pharmuthi, 4th	13 July	Mesore.	20 May	Pharmuthi.	26 May	Payni.
	18 July (Five days added)	Five days added.	20 June	Pachon.	25 June	Epiphi.
			19 July		25 July	

Natural Year seasons: Season of Inundation. — Season of Vegetation. — Season of Drought.

In the first column of the accompanying Table explaining the Egyptian Calendar, we have the names of the months, together with their hieroglyphical descriptions, as belonging to the several seasons.

In the second column we have the three seasons of the year, each divided into four months, with the days on which those seasons were supposed by the Egyptians to begin, and also the days on which each of the twelve months would always have begun if the Egyptians had known the true length of the year, and had understood how to regulate the civil year by the help of intercalary days.

The third column shows how, according to Censorinus, the year was arranged at the beginning of the Sothic Period, B.C. 1322, called by Theon the Era of Menophra. At that time, perhaps, the five additional days, called the Epagomenæ, were added to the twelve months of thirty days each, under the belief that the year consisted of 365 days, and that the months would for the future remain stationary, each keeping to its own season. It will be observed that the months did not then pictorially represent the seasons in which they fell. Thus Thoth, which began on the 18th of July, when the inundation began, is pictorially the first month of vegetation. Each of the months, so far as its name was pictorial, was the third part of the year out of place.

Of course, with the want of an intercalary day on every fourth year, the months did not remain fixed to their seasons; and the fourth column represents the Egyptian Calendar at the date of this Decree, when the priests proposed to introduce the intercalary day every fourth year, and to check the wandering of the months for the future. This column is confirmed by the words of the Decree, which, in lines 37 and 38 of the Greek, informs us that the month of Payni began with the heliacal rising of the Dog Star, and with the beginning of the Nile's overflow—that is to say, about the 18th of July.

The praiseworthy wish of the priests was, however, not carried into effect. The intercalary day was not introduced into the calendar, and the civil New-year's day continued to wander through the seasons. Our fifth column represents the civil year in the year B.C. 25, when Augustus enforced the wishes of Julius Cæsar in Alexandria, and introduced the system of intercalating one day every four years. From that time forward the Alexandrian year ceased to be movable. It began on the 29th of August; while the Egyptian year continued to wander round the seasons as before.

The last three columns in our Table are again and again confirmed by records of the astronomical observations in the writings of Claudius Ptolemy, and Theon. For the Alexandrian astronomers, following in the steps of their Babylonian brethren, always made use of the movable year of 365 days, which was much more certain to be hereafter understood than the new Julian year, which, having been made by the edict of one emperor, might easily be altered by another.

Our Decree is dated the 9th year of Euergetes, or B.C. 238; and C. Ptolemy has preserved for us two astronomical records of about that time, which satisfactorily prove when the Egyptian months began, and also when the Macedonian month Apellæus began. In the year B.C. 244, the 5th of Apellæus was the 27th of Thoth; or Apellæus began on 23rd of Thoth, our 14th of November. Eight years later, in the year B.C. 236, the 14th of Dius was the 9th of Thoth, and Apellæus, the next month, began on the 26th of Thoth, our 15th of November. The difference of the one day is not easily explained, because of the uncertainty as to the intercalation in the Macedonian year, which need not here be entered upon.

The above records also show that in the year B.C. 244, Thoth began on the 23rd of October, and that in the year B.C. 236, it began on the 21st of October, very exactly confirming our fourth column, where, in the year B.C. 238, the 1st of Thoth is placed on the 22nd of October; and also confirming those words of the Decree, which place the 1st of Payni about the 19th July.

If we now, with this knowledge, turn to the date of the Decree, we shall find that the priests, by the month of Tybi, mean, not the Tybi of the civil year then in use, which began on the 19th of February, but the Tybi of the reformed Calendar which they are thus proposing to introduce. The first line of our Decree makes Tybi begin ten days before Apellæus, that is, in some time in November. It would not be easy to say exactly what day of November the priests would then place the 1st of Tybi, from the uncertainty, as before remarked, in the intercalation of the Macedonian year; but it is clear that they proposed that Tybi should stand very nearly as it does in our third column, when Thoth began with the rising of the Dog Star, as arranged at the Era of Menophra. In the date of the Decree, the month Tybi is clearly not that in our fourth column, the civil year then in use, but that in our third column, the civil year of Menophra, B.C. 1322, and of A.D. 138, when, after the lapse of four times 365 years, the Egyptian New-year's day had again returned to its original place in the natural year.

Plate I.   lines 1–3.

DECREE OF CANOPUS.

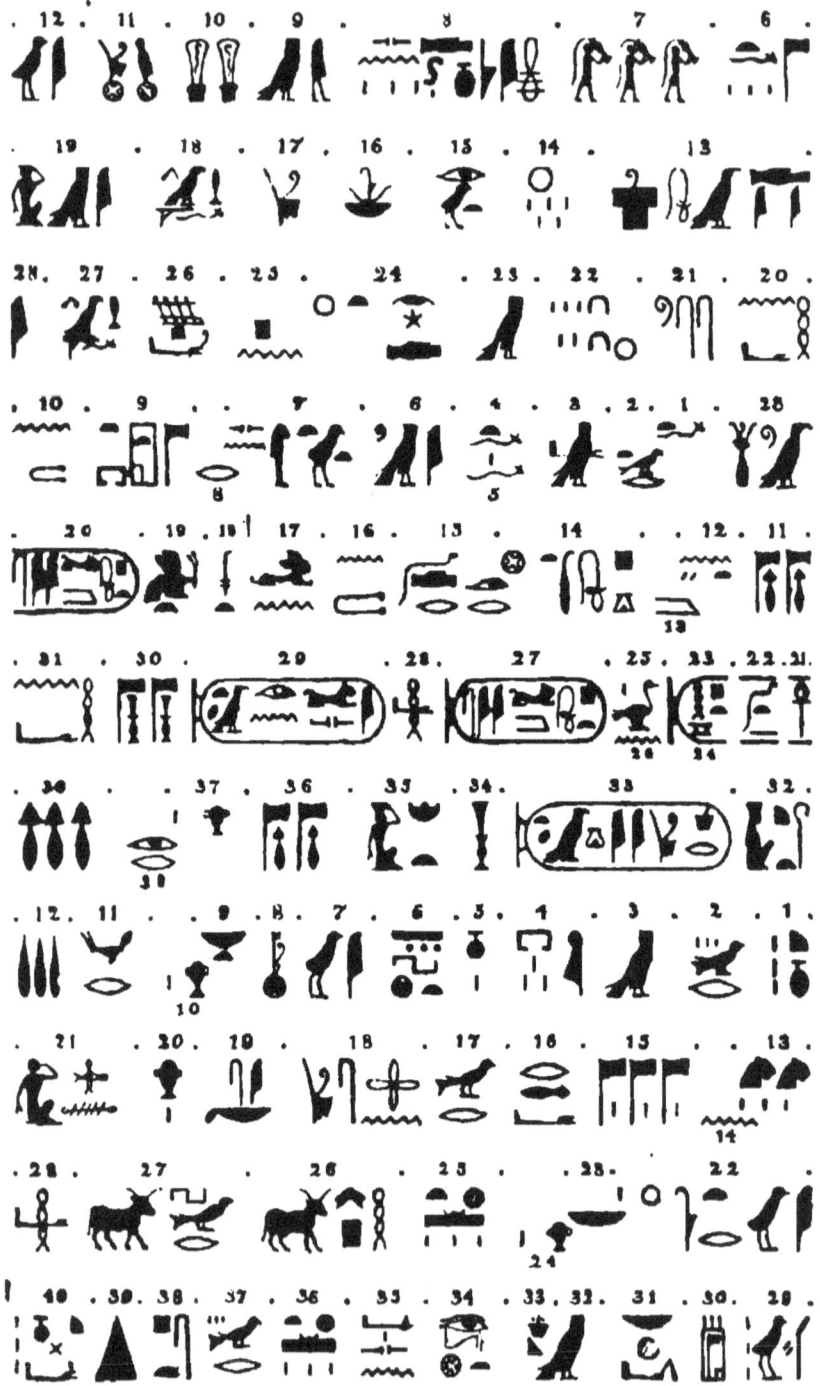

Plate 3.   DECREE OF CANOPUS.   lines 6-8.

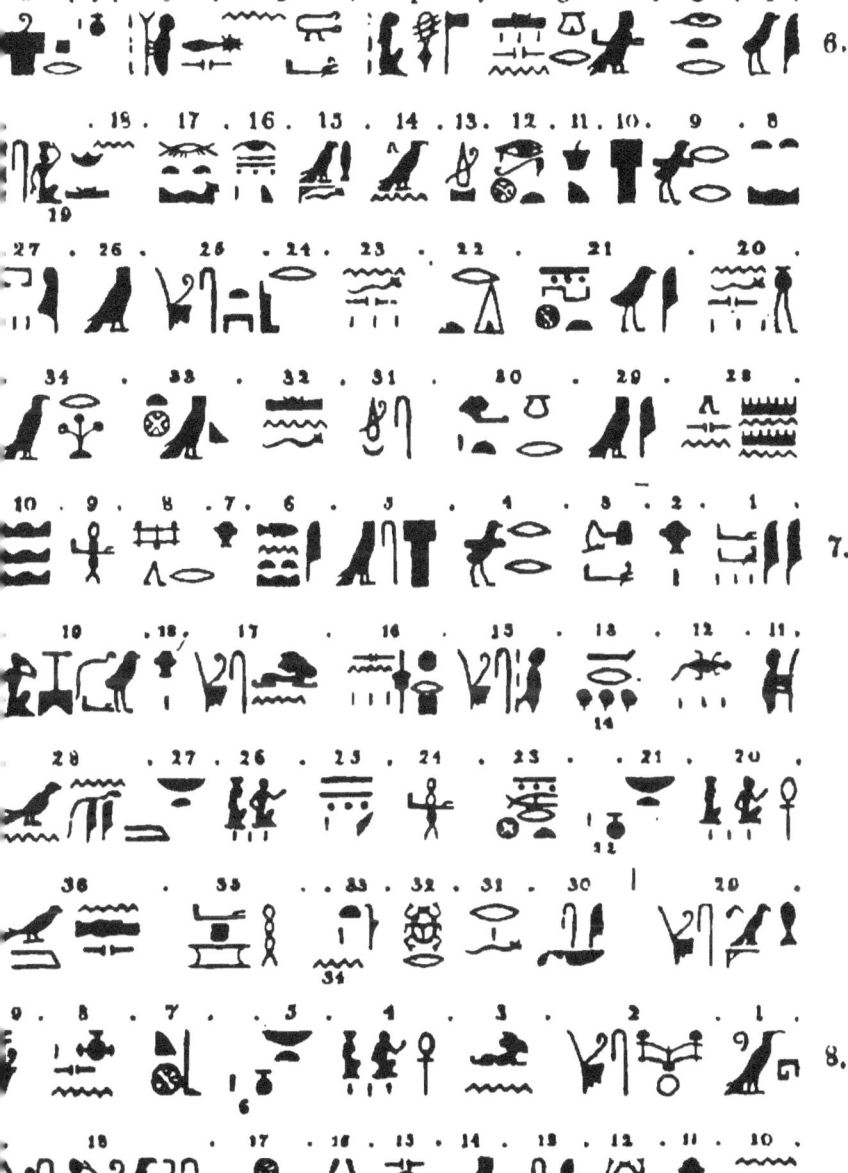

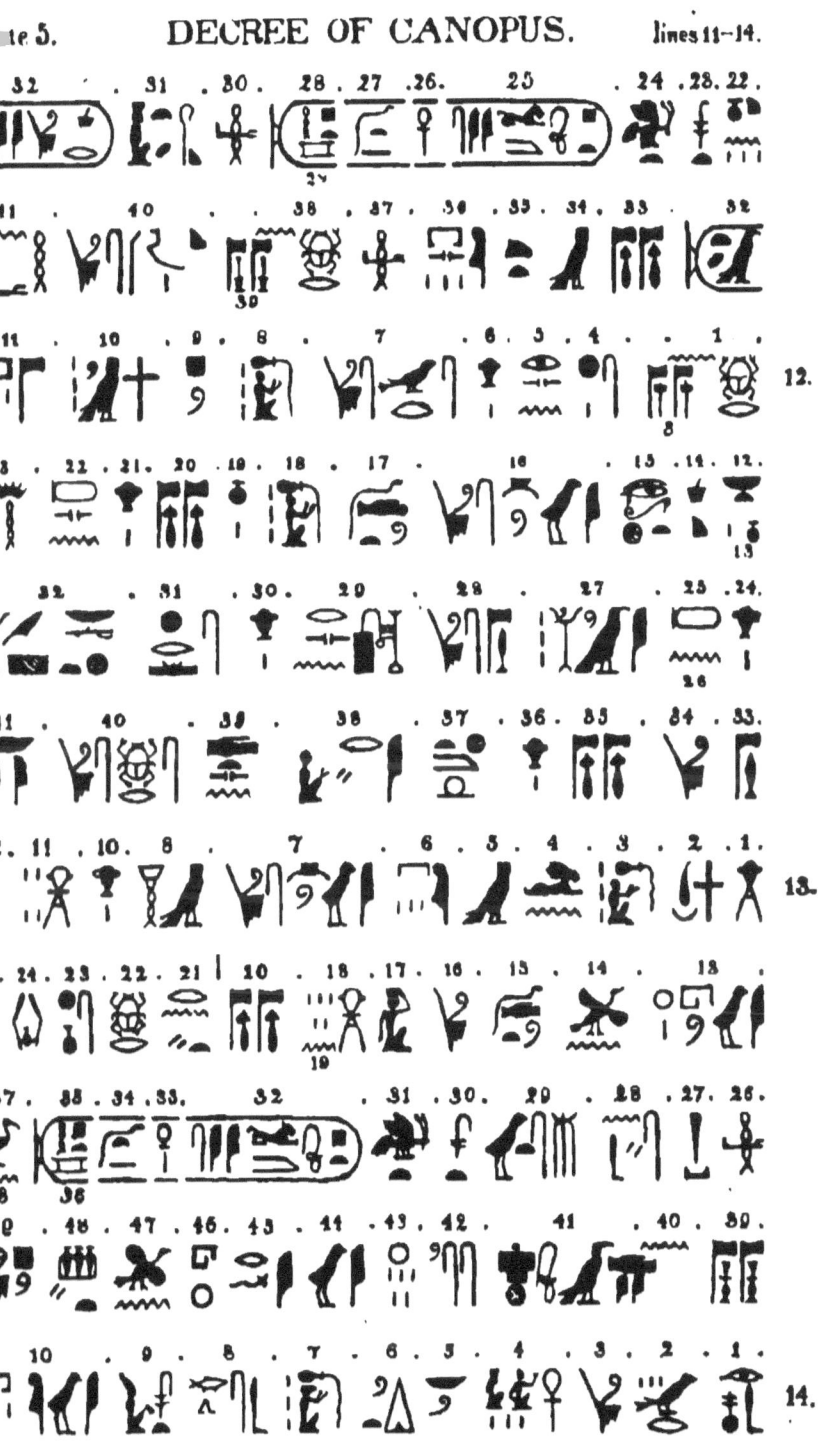

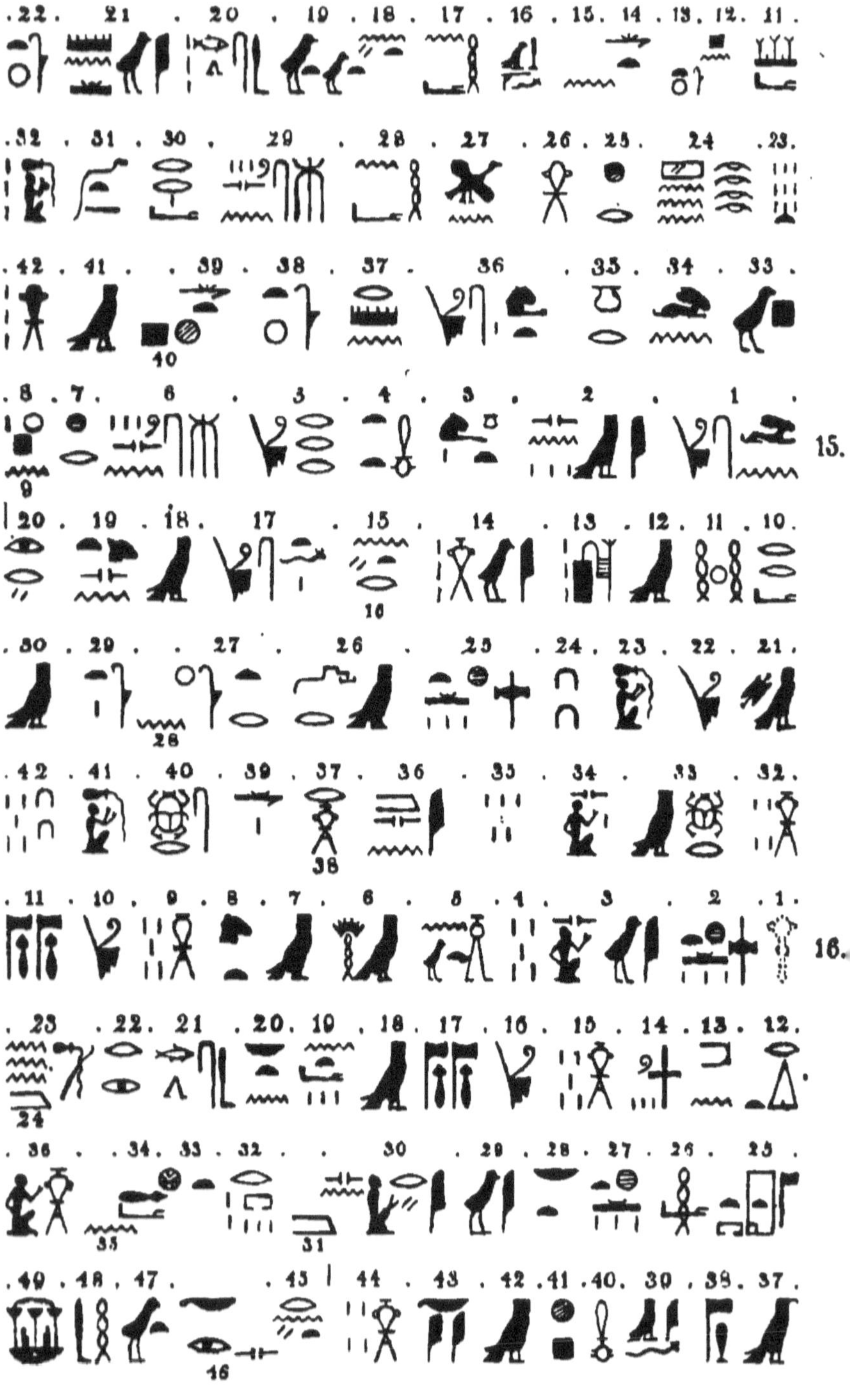
15.
16.

Plate 7.   DECREE OF CANOPUS.   lines 17–19.

13 . 12 . 11 . 10 . 9 . 7 . 6 . 5 . 4 . 3 . 2 . 1.

17.

24 . 23 . 22 . 21 . 20 . 19 . 18 . 17 . 16 . 15 . 14.

33 . 32 . 31 . 30 . 29 . 28 . 27 . 26 . 25.

43 . 42 . 41 . 40 . 39 . 38 . 37 . 36 . 35 . 34.
44

8 . 7 . 6 . 5 . 4 . 3 . 2 . 1.

18.

22 . 21 . 20 . 19 . 18 . 17 . 16 . 15 . 14 . 13 . 11 . 10.
12

33 . 32 . 30 . 29 . 28 . 27 . 26 . 25 . 24 . 23.
31

47 . 46 . 45 . 43 . 42 . 11 . 40 . 39 . 38 . 37 . 36 . 35 . 34.
44

9 . 8 . 7 . 6 . 5 . 2 . 1.

19.

21 . 20 . 19 . 18 . 16 . 14 . 13 . 12 . 11 . 10.
17   18

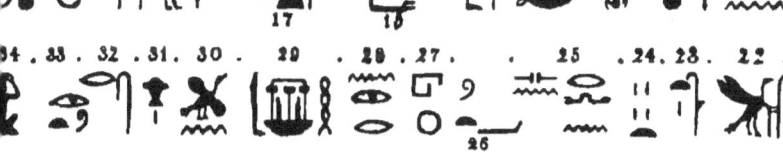

34 . 33 . 32 . 31 . 30 . 29 . 28 . 27 . 25 . 24 . 23 . 22.
26

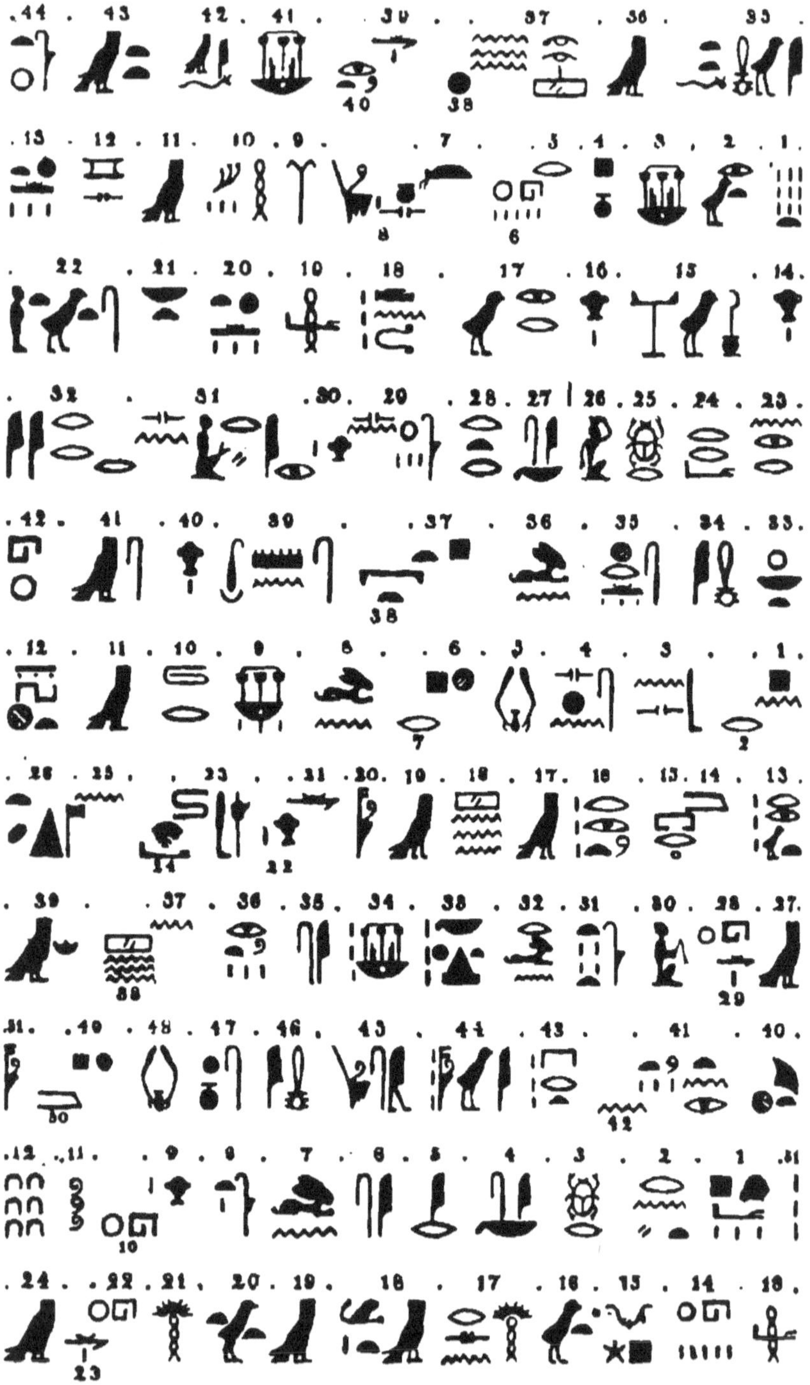

Plate 9. DECREE OF CANOPUS. lines 22-25.

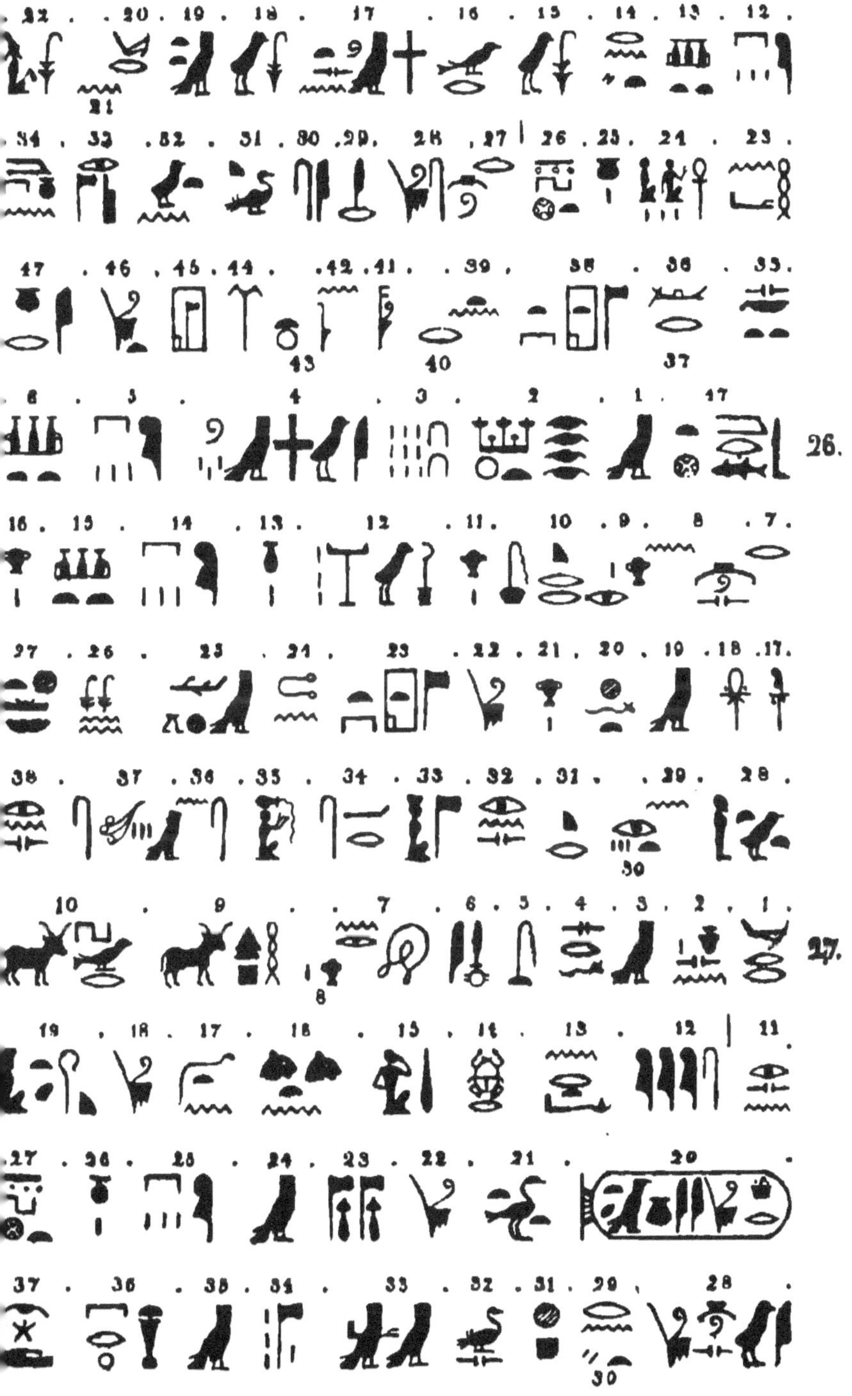
26.
27.

Plate 11.   DECREE OF CANOPUS.   lines 28-30.

42 . 41 . 40 . 39 . . 37 . 36 . 35 .

38

13 . 12 . 11 . 10 . 9 . 8 . 7 . 6 . 5 | 4 . . 3 . . 2 . 1.   31.

. 23 . 22 . 21 . 20 . 19 . . 17 . 16 . 15 . 14 .

24   18 -

31 . 30 . 29 . 28 . 27 . 26 . 25 . 24 .

45 44 . 43 . 42 . 41 . . 40 . 39 . 38 . 37 . 36 . 35 . 34 . 33 . 32.

13 . 12 . . 10 . 9 . 8 . 7 . 6 . . 4 . 3 . 2 . 1 . 45   32.

11   5

24 . 23 . 22 . 21 . 20 . 19 | 18 . 17 . 16 . 15 . 14 .

35 . 34 . 33 . 32 . 31 . 30 . 29 . 28 . 27 . 26 . 25 .

45 . 44 . 43 . 42 . 41 . 40 . 39 . 38 . 37 . 36 .

12 . 11 . 10 . 9 . 8 . 7 | 6 . 5 . 4 . 3 . 2 . 1   33.

24 . 23 . 22 . 21 . 20 . 19 . 18 . 17 . 16 . 15 . 14 . 13 .

Plate 13.   DECREE OF CANOPUS.   lines 33-36.

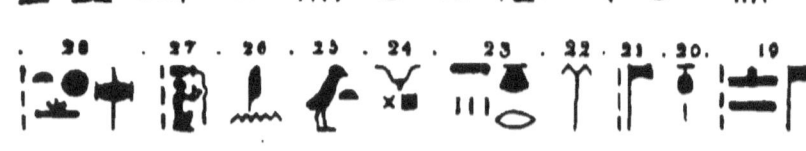

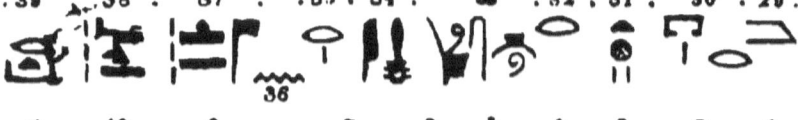

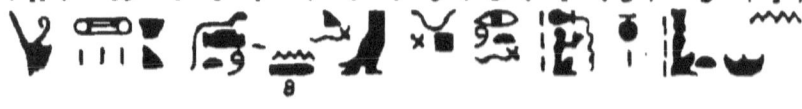

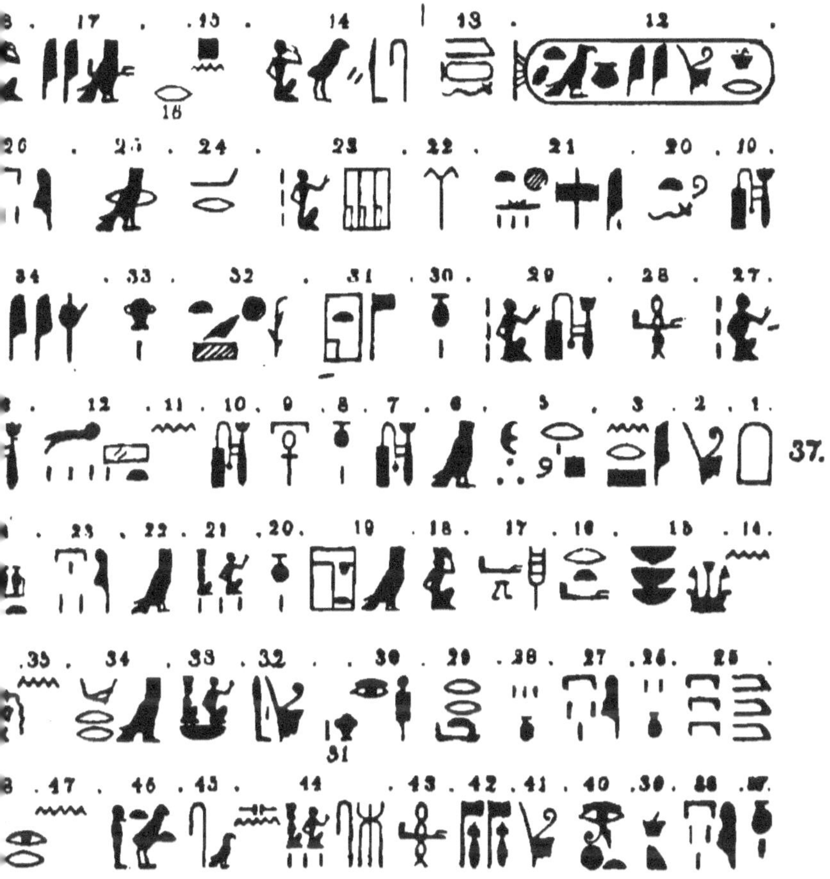

Plate 15.

ALPHABET.

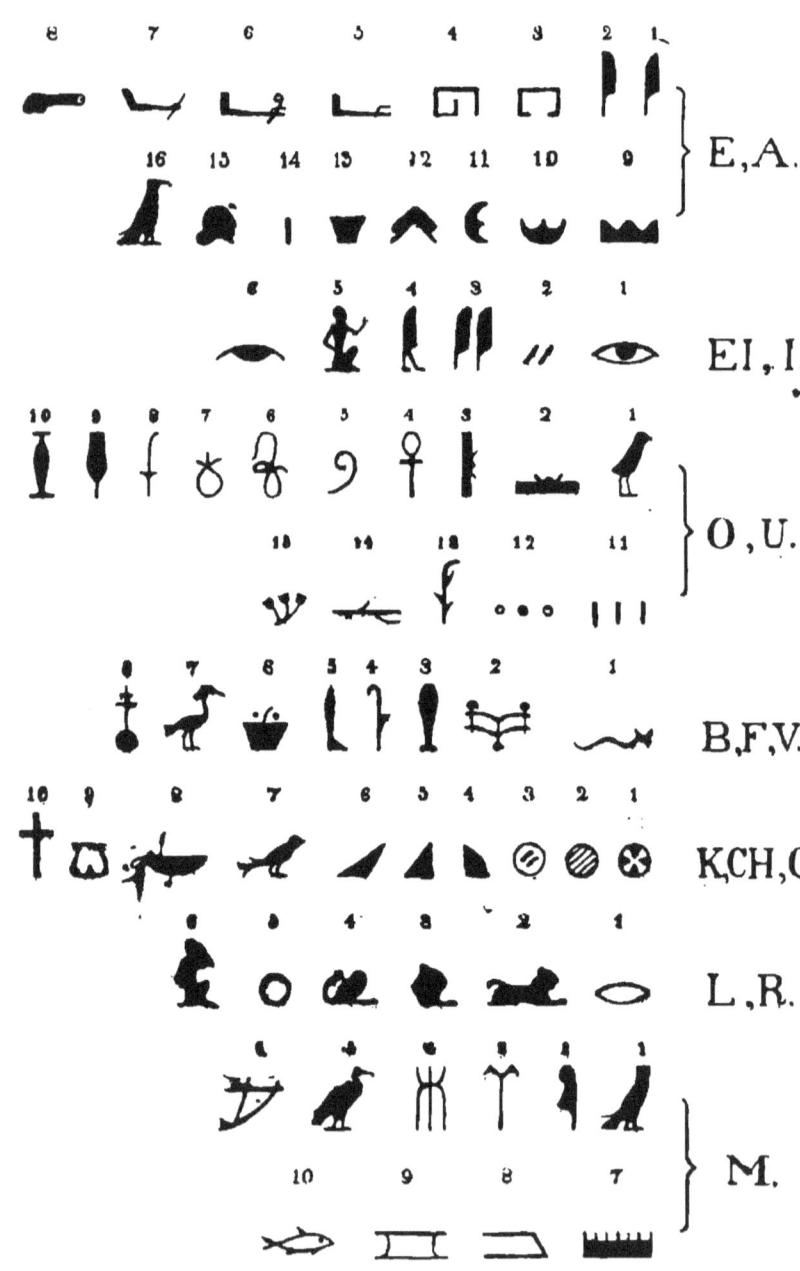

Plate 16.

ALPHABET.

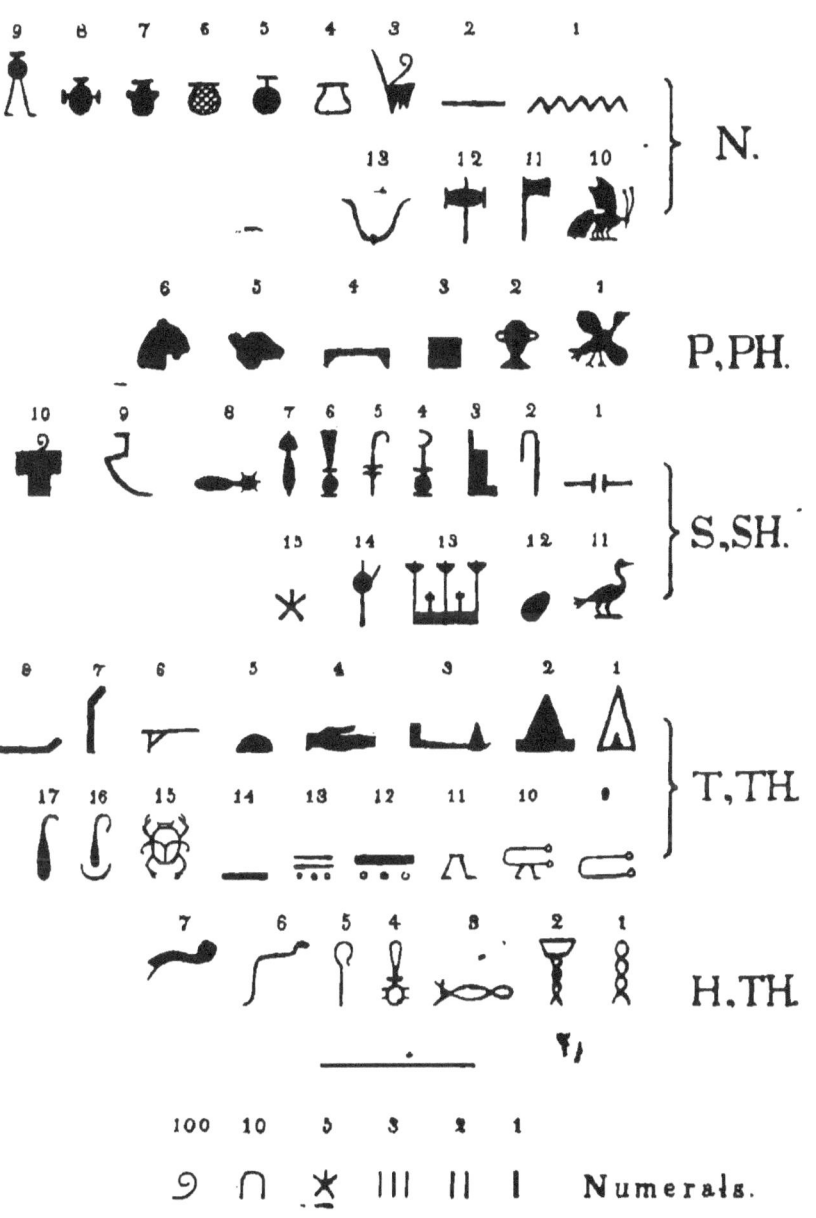

DECREE OF CANOPUS.

Lines 1—10.]

1 Βασιλευοντος Πτολεμαιου του Πτολεμαιου και Αρσινοης,
θεων Αδελφων, ετους ενατου, εφ᾽ ιερεως Απολλωνιδου του

2 Μοσχιωνος Αλεξανδρου και θεων Αδελφων και θεων
Ευεργετων, κανηφορου Αρσινοης Φιλαδελφου Μενεκρατειας

3 της Φιλαμμονος, μηνος Απελλαιου ἑβδομη, Αιγυπτιων δε
Τυβι ἑπτακαιδεκατη.—Ψηφισμα.— Οἱ αρχιερεις

4 και προφηται και οἱ εις το᾽ αδυτον εισπορευομενοι προς τον
στολισμον των θεων και πτεροφοραι και ιερογραμματεις και

5 οἱ αλλοι ιερεις οἱ συναντησαντες εκ των κατα την χωραν
ιερων εις την πεμπτην του Διου, εν ᾗ αγεται τα γενεθλια του

6 βασιλεως, και εις την πεμπτην και εικαδα του αυτου μηνος,
εν ᾗ παρελαβεν την βασιλειαν παρα του πατρος, συν-
εδρευσαντες

7 ταυτῃ τῃ ἡμερᾳ εν τῳ εν Κανωπῳ ιερῳ των Ευεργετων
θεων ειπαν· Επειδη βασιλευς Πτολεμαιος Πτολεμαιου και
Αρσινοης, θεων Αδελφων,

8 και βασιλισσα Βερενικη, ἡ αδελφη αυτου και γυνη, θεοι
Ευεργεται, διατελουσιν πολλα και μεγαλα ευεργετουντες τα
κατα την χωραν ιερα και

9 τας τιμας των θεων επι πλεον αυξοντες, του τε Απιος και
του Μνηυιος και των λοιπων ενλογιμων ιερων ζῳων των εν
τῃ χωρᾳ την

10 επιμελειαν δια᾽παντος ποιουνται μετα μεγαλης δαπανης και
χορηγιας και τα εξενεγχθεντα εκ της χωρας ιερα αγαλματα
ὑπο

B

11 των Περσων εξστρατευσας ὁ βασιλευς ανεσωσεν εις Αιγυπτον
και απεδωκεν εις τα ἱερα, ὁθεν ἑκαστον εξ αρχης εξηχθη,
την τε

12 χωραν εν ειρηνη διατετηρηκεν, προπολεμων ὑπερ αυτης προς
πολλα εθνη και τους εν αυτοις δυναστευοντας, και τοις εν
τη χωρα

13 πασιν και τοις αλλοις τοις ὑπο την αυτων βασιλειαν
τασσομενοις την ευνομιαν παρεχουσιν, του τε ποταμου ποτε
ελλιπεστερον ανα-

14 βαντος και παντων των εν τη χωρα καταπεπληγμενων επι
τω συμβεβηκοτι, και ενθυμουμενων την γεγενημενην
καταφθοραν

15 επι τινων των προτερον βεβασιλευκοτων, εφ' ὡν συνεβη
αβροχιαις περιπεπτωκεναι τους την χωραν κατοικουντας,
προσταντες κηδεμο-

16 νικως των τε εν τοις ἱεροις και των αλλων των την χωραν
κατοικουντων πολλα μεν προνοηθεντες, ουκ ολιγας δε των
προσοδων ὑπερ-

17 ιδοντες ἑνεκα της των ανθρωπων σωτηριας, εκ τε Συριας και
Φοινικης και Κυπρου και εξ αλλων πλειονων τοπων σιτον
μεταπεμ-

18 ψαμενοι εις την χωραν τιμων μειζονων, διεσωσαν τους την
Αιγυπτον κατοικουντας, αθανατον ευεργεσιαν και της αυτων
αρετης

19 μεγιστον ὑπομνημα καταλειποντες τοις τε νυν ουσιν και τοις
επιγινομενοις, ανθ' ὡν οἱ θεοι δεδωκασιν αυτοις ευσταθουσαν
την βασιλει-

20 αν και δωσουσιν τἀλλ' αγαθα παντα εις τον αει χρονον·--
Αγαθη Τυχη·-- Δεδοχθαι τοις κατα την χωραν ἱερευσιν τας
τε προυπαρχουσας

21 τιμας εν τοις ἱεροις βασιλει Πτολεμαιω και βασιλισση
Βερενικη, θεοις Ευεργεταις, και τοις γονευσιν αυτων, θεοις
Αδελφοις, και τοις προγονοις,

22 θεοις Σωτηρσιν, αυξειν και τους ιερεις τους εν εκαστω των
κατα την χωραν ιερων προσονομαζεσθαι ιερεις και των
Ευεργετων θεων και ενγραφε·

23 σθαι εν πασιν τοις χρηματισμοις και εν τοις δακτυλιοις,
ους φορουσιν, προσεγκολαπτεσθαι και την ιερωσυνην των
Ευεργετων θεων· προσαποδειχθη·

24 ναι δε προς ταις νυν υπαρχουσαις τεσσαρσι φυλαις του
πληθους των ιερεων των εν εκαστω ιερω και αλλην, η
προσονομασθησεται πεμ·

25 πτη φυλη των Ευεργετων θεων, επει και συν τη αγαθη τυχη
και την γενεσιν βασιλεως Πτολεμαιου του των θεων Αδελφων
συμβεβηκεν

26 γενεσθαι τη πεμπτη του Διου, η και πολλων αγαθων
αρχηγετον εν πασιν ανθρωποις· εις δε την φυλην ταυτην
καταλεχθηναι τους απο

27 του πρωτου ετους γεγενημενους ιερεις και τους προσκαταγη-
σομενους εως μηνος Μεσορη του εν τω ενατω ετει και τους
τουτων εκγονους εις τον αει

28 χρονον τους δε προυπαρχοντας ιερεις εως του πρωτου ετους
ειναι ωσαυτως εν ταις αυταις φυλαις, εν αις προτερον ησαν,
ως δε και τους

29 εκγονους αυτων απο του νυν καταχωριζεσθαι εις τας αυτας
φυλας, εν αις οι πατερες εισιν· αντι δε των εικοσι βουλευτων
ιερεων των νυν αιρουμενων

30 κατ᾽ ενιαυτον εκ των προυπαρχουσων τεσσαρων φυλων, εξ
ων πεντε αφ᾽ εκαστης φυλης λαμβανονται, εικοσι και πεντε
τους βουλευτας

31 ιερεις ειναι, προσλαμβανομενων εκ της πεμπτης φυλης των
Ευεργετων θεων αλλων πεντε· μετεχειν δε και τους εκ της
πεμπτης

32 φυλης των Ευεργετων θεων των αγνειων και των αλλων
απαντων των εν τοις ιεροις και φυλαρχον αυτης ειναι καθ᾽ α
και επι των αλλων τεσ-

33 σαρων φυλων ὑπαρχει· και επειδη καθ᾽ ἑκαστον μηνα αγοντα
εν τοις ἱεροις ἑορται των Ευεργετων θεων κατα το προτερο
ψηφισμα

34 ἡ τε πεμπτη και ἡ ενατη και ἡ πεμπτη επ᾽ εικαδι, τοις τ
αλλοις μεγιστοις θεοις κατ᾽ ενιαυτον συντελουνται ἑορται κα
πανηγυρεις δημοτε·

35 λεις, αγεσθαι κατ᾽ ενιαυτον πανηγυριν δημοτελη εν τε τοι
ἱεροις και καθ᾽ ὁλην την χωραν βασιλει Πτολεμαιω κα
βασιλισση Βερενικη,

36 θεοις Ευεργεταις, τη. ἡμερᾳ, εν ᾗ επιτελλει το αστρον το τη
Ισιος, ἡ νομιζεται δια των ἱερων γραμματων νεον ετος ειναι
αγεται δε νυν, εν τῳ

37 ενατῳ ετει. νουμηνιᾳ του Παυνι μηνος, εν ᾧ και τα μικρ
Βουβαστια και τα μεγαλα Βουβαστια αγεται και ἡ συναγωγ
των καρπων και ἡ του

38 ποταμου αναβασις γινεται· εαν δε και συμβαινη τη
επιτολην του αστρου μεταβαινειν εις ἑτεραν ἡμεραν δι
τεσσαρων ετων, μη μετατι-

39 θεσθαι την πανηγυριν, αλλ᾽ αγεσθαι τη νουμηνιᾳ του Παυν
εν ᾗ και εξ αρχης ηχθη εν τῳ ετει, και συντελειν αυτην επ
ἡμερας

40 πεντε μετα στεφανηφοριας και θυσιων και σπονδων και τω
αλλων των προσηκοντων· ὁπως δε και αἱ ὡραι το καθηκο
ποιωσι δια παντος κατα την νυν

41 καταστασιν του κοσμου και μη συμβαινη τινας των δημοτελω
ἑορτων των αγομενων εν τῳ χειμονι αγεσθαι ποτε εν τ
θερει, του αστρου

42 μεταβαινοντος μιαν ἡμεραν δια τεσσαρων ετων, ἑτερας δ
των νυν αγομενων εν τῳ θερει αγεσθαι εν τῳ χειμονι εν το
μετα ταυτα καιροις, καθαπερ προ-

43 τερον τε συμβεβηκεν γενεσθαι κἀνυν ανεγινετο, της συνταξεω
του ενιαυτου μενουσης εκ των τριακοσιων και ἑξηκοντ
ἡμερων και των ὑστερον προσ·

44 νομισθεισων επαγεσθαι πεντε ἡμερων, απο του νυν μιαν
ἡμεραν ἑορτην των Ευεργετων θεων επαγεσθαι δια τεσσαρων
ετων επι ταις πεντε ταις

45 επαγομεναις προ του νεου ετους, ὁπως ἁπαντες ειδωσιν, διοτι
το ελλειπον προτερον περι την συνταξιν των ὡρων και του
ενιαυτου, και των νομιζο-

46 μενων περι την ὁλην διακοσμησιν του πολου διωρθωσθαι και
αναπεπληρωσθαι συμβεβηκεν δια των Ευεργετων θεων· και
επειδη την εκ βασιλεως Πτολεμαιου

47 και βασιλισσης Βερενικης, θεων Ευεργετων, γεγενημενην
θυγατερα και ονομασθεισαν Βερενικην, ἡ και βασιλισσα
ευθεως απεδειχθη, συνεβη ταυτην παρθενον

48 ὡς αν εξαιφνης μετελθειν εις τον αεναον κοσμον ετι
ενδημουντων παρα τῳ βασιλει των εκ της χωρας
παραγινομενων προς αυτον κατ᾽ ενιαυτον ἱερεων,

49 οἱ μεγα πενθος επι τῳ συμβεβηκοτι ευθεως συνετελεσαν
αξιωσαντες τε τον βασιλεα και την βασιλισσαν επεισαν
καθιδρυσαι την θεαν μετα του Οσιριος εν τῳ

50 εν Κανωπῳ ἱερῳ, ὁ ου μονον εν τοις πρωτοις ἱεροις εστιν,
αλλα και ὑπο του βασιλεως και των κατα την χωραν παντων
εν τοις μαλιστα τιμωμενοις ὑπαρχει·

51 και ἡ αναγωγη του ἱερου πλοιου του Οσειριος εις τουτο το
ἱερον κατ᾽ ενιαυτον γινεται εκ του εν τῳ Ἡρακλειῳ ἱερου τῃ
ενατῃ και εικαδι του Χοιαχ, των του δρομου

52 των ἱερων παντων θυσιας συντελουντων επι των ιδρυμενων
ὑπ᾽ αυτων βωμων ὑπερ ἑκαστου ἱερου των πρωτων εξ
αμφοτερων των μερων του δρομου·

53 μετα δε ταυτα προς την εκθεωσιν αυτης νομιμα και την του
πενθους απολυσιν απεδωκαν μεγαλοπρεπως και κηδεμονικως
καθαπερ επι τῳ Απιι

54 και Μνηυιει, οἱς μεν ενεστιν γινεσθαι. Δεδοχθαι συντελειν
τῃ εκ των Ευεργετων θεων γεγενημενῃ, βασιλισσῃ, Βερενικῃ,
τιμας αιδιους εν ὑπασι των

55 κατα την χωραν ἱεροις· και επει εις θεους μετηλθεν εν τῳ
Τυβι μηνι, εν ᾡπερ και ἡ του Ἡλιου θυγατηρ εν αρχῃ
μετηλλαξεν τον βιον, ἡν ὁ πατηρ στησας ονο-

56 μασεν ὁτε μεν βασιλειαν ὁτε ὁρασιν αυτου, και αγουσιν
αυτῃ ἑορτην και περιπλουν εν πλειοσιν ἱεροις των πρωτων
εν τουτῳ τῳ μηνι εν ᾡ ἡ αποθεωσις αυτης

57 εν αρχῃ εγενηθη, συντελειν και βασιλισσῃ Βερενικῃ τῃ εκ
των Ευεργετων θεων εν ἁπασι τοις κατα την χωραν ἱεροις εν
τῳ Τυβι μηνι ἑορτην και πε-

58 ριπλουν εις ἡμερας τεσσαρας απο ἑπτακαιδεκατης, εν ᾑ ὁ
περιπλους και ἡ του πενθους απολυσις εγενηθη αυτῃ την
αρχην· συντελεσαι δ' αυτης και

59 ἱερον αγαλμα χρυσουν διαλιθον εν ἑκαστῳ των πρωτων και
δευτερων ἱερων και καθιδρυσαι εν τῳ ἁγιῳ· ὁ δε προφητης
μετα των εις το αδυτον ερχομενων

60 ἱερεων προς τον στολισμον των θεων οιση εν ταις αγκαλαις,
ὁταν αἱ εξοδειαι και πανηγυρεις των λοιπων θεων γινωνται,
ὁπως ὑπο παντων ὁρωμενον

61 τιμαται και προσκυνηται καλουμενον Βερενικης, ανασσης
παρθενων· ειναι δε την επιτιθεμενην βασιλειαν τῃ εικονι
αυτης διαφερουσαν της επιτιθεμενης

62 ταις εικοσιν της μητρος αυτης, βασιλισσης Βερενικης, εκ
σταχυων δυων, ὡν αναμεσον εσται ἡ ασπιδοειδης βασιλεια,
ταυτης δ' οπισω συμμετρον σκηπτρον

63 παπυροειδες. ὁ δ' ειωθασιν αἱ θεαι εχειν εν ταις χερσιν· περι
οὑ και ἡ ουρα της βασιλειας εσται περιειλημμενη, ὡστε και
εκ της διαθεσεως της βασιλειας δια-

64 σαφεισθαι το Βερενικης ονομα κατα τα επισημα της ἱερας
γραμματικης· και ὁταν τα Κικηλλια αγηται εν τῳ Χοιαχ
μηνι προ του περιπλου του Οσειριος, κατα-

65 σκευασαι τας παρθενους των ἱερεων αλλο αγαλμα Βερενικης,
ανασσης παρθενων, ᾡ συντελεσουσιν ὁμοιως θυσιαν και
ταλλα τα συντελουμενα νο-

66 μιμα τη έορτη ταυτη· εξειναι δε κατα ταυτα και ταις αλλαις
παρθενοις ταις βουλομεναις συντελειν τα νομιμα τη θεῳ,
ὑμνεισθαι δ᾽ αυτην και ὑ·

67 πο των επιλεγομενων ἱερειων παρθενων και τας χρειας
παρεχομενων τοις θεοις, περικειμενων ται ιδιας βασιλειας
των θεων, [ὡν] ἱερειαι νομιζονται

68 ειναι· και ὁταν ὁ προωριμος σπορος παραστῃ, αναφερειν τας
ἱερας παρθενους σταχυς τους παραθησομενους τῳ αγαλματι
της θεου, ᾀδειν δ᾽ εις αυτην

69 καθ᾽ ἡμεραν και εν ταις ἑορταις και πανηγυρεσιν των λοιπων
θεων τους τε ᾠδους ανδρας και τας γυναικας, ους αν ὑμνους
οἱ ἱερογραμματεις γρα-

70 ψαντες δωσιν τῳ ᾠδοδιδασκαλῳ, ὡν και τὰντιγραφα κατα-
χωρισθησεται εις τας ἱερας βιβλους· και επειδη τοις ἱερευσιν
διδονται αἱ τροφαι εκ των

71 ἱερων, επαν επαχθωσιν εις το πληθος, διδοσθαι ταις
θυγατρασιν των ἱερεων εκ των ἱερων προσοδων, αφ᾽ ἡς αν
ἡμερας γενωνται, την συνκριθησομε-

72 νην τροφην ὑπο των βουλευτων ἱερεων των εν ἑκαστῳ των
ἱερων κατα λογον των ἱερων προσοδων, και τον διδομενον
αρτον ταις γυναιξιν

73 των ἱερεων εχειν διον τυπον και καλεισθαι Βερενικης αρτον·
ὁ δ᾽ εν ἑκαστῳ των ἱερων κατεστηκως επιστατης και αρχιερευς
και οἱ του ἱερου

74 γραμματεις αναγραψατωσαν τουτο ψηφισμα εις στηλην
λιθινην η χαλκην ἱεροις γραμμασιν και Αιγυπτιοις και
Ἑλληνικοις και αναθε-

75 τωσαν εν τῳ επιφανεστατῳ τοπῳ των τε πρωτων ἱερων και
δευτερων και τριτων, ὁπως οἱ κατα την χωραν ἱερεις φαι-
νωνται τιμωντας τους Ευεργετας θεους και τα τεκνα αυτων,

76 καθαπερ δικαιον εστιν.

DECREE OF CANOPUS,

FROM THE GREEK.

[Lines 1—11.

1 In the reign of Ptolemy the *son* of Ptolemy and of Arsinoe, the brother-gods, in the ninth year [B.C. 238], under Apollonides
2 the son of Moschion the priest of Alexander, and of the brother-gods, and of the gods Euergetæ, and Menecratein the daughter of
3 Philammon the basket-bearer of Arsinoe Philadelphus, on the seventh *day* of the month Apellaius, and the seventeenth of Tybi according to the Egyptians, a Decree;

4 The chief priests, and prophets, and those who enter the sanctuary for the robing of the gods, and the feather-bearers, and sacred
5 scribes, and the other priests who had met together out of the temples throughout the country for the fifth *day* of Dius, on
6 which is kept the birthday of the king, and for the twenty-fifth *day* of the same month on which he received the kingdom from
7 his father, having met in council together on that day in the temple of the gods Euergetæ, which is in Canopus, declared;

Whereas King Ptolemy, the son of Ptolemy and Arsinoe the
8 brother-gods, and Queen Berenice his sister and wife, the gods Euergetæ, continue in many and great things benefiting the
9 temples throughout the country; and the honours of the gods they have yet further increased; and of Apis and Mnevis, and of the other celebrated animals which are in the country they take
10 great care, with great cost and ceremonial expenditure;

And the sacred images which had been carried out of the
11 country by the Persians, the king having made war, brought safe into Egypt, and gave back to the temples whence each had

DECREE OF CANOPUS,

FROM THE HIEROGLYPHICS.

Lines 1—6.]

1 *In the* year ninth, *in the month of* Apellaius upon *the* day seven,
of Tybi seventeen according to *the* Egyptians, *in the* reign *of*
King Ptolemy, living *for* ever, beloved *by* Pthah, son *of* Ptolemy
and of Arsinoe brother-gods, *when the* priest of Alexander deceased
2 and *of the* brother-gods, and *of the* gods Euergetæ *was* Apollonides
the *son* of Moschion, and Menecrateia *the* daughter *of* Philammon
was basket-bearer *for* Arsinoe loving *her* brother, on that day, a
Writing;

The chief priests *of the* temples, *the* high-priests, *the* guardians
3 of the temples, the purifiers, those who sing hymns, those who
robe *the gods*, the writers of the sacred books, the other
divine prophets, having purified themselves, being assembled
together, having come from *the* two provinces *of* Upper *and* Lower
Egypt, *for the* fifth day *of* Dius, *when* the anniversary day of his
majesty was celebrated, likewise upon *the* twenty fifth-day of that
4 month *when* his majesty received his great kingdom from his
father, having celebrated religious honours in *the* temple of *the*
gods Euergetæ, which *is* in Canopus, declared this Decree;

King Ptolemy living *for* ever, beloved *by* Pthah, son of Ptolemy
and *of* Arsinoe *the* brother-gods, likewise Queen Berenice *his* sister
5 and wife, *the* gods Euergetæ; he made columns *with* great
expense for all *the* temples of *the* country *of* Egypt, he prepared
obelisks, colossal statues, for *the* gods, *with* great abundance *of*
things fit, when, behold, he supplied all *the* other yearly things for
the bull Apis *and the* bull Mnevis, and *the* animals *in the* temples,
regulating in *the* cities *of* Egypt *with* other great gifts, excellent
gifts *of* revenues;
6 And that *he* might make re-conquest *of the* sacred images
which had been captured *by the* barbarians of Persia, *he* made
war on behalf of *the* cities *of* Egypt *with* good fortune; his

12 been at first taken away, and hath kept the country in peace,
   carrying war on its behalf against many nations, and those who
13 have power in them; and to all those in the country, and to all
   others under their dominion, they render justice;

14   And once when the Nile rose rather insufficiently, and all those
   in the country were struck down by what had happened, and
15 were considering the calamity that had happened, under some of
   the former sovereigns, under whom it happened that those who
   inhabited the country were ruined by the drought, standing
16 forward carefully, having forethought in many things for those
   in the temples, and the others who inhabit the country,

17 and overlooking not a few of the taxes for the welfare of the men,
   out of Syria, and Phenicia, and Cyprus, and many other places,
18 having sent for corn, into the country at great expense, they saved
   the inhabitants of Egypt,

19 leaving immortal beneficence and a very great memory of their
   virtue, both to those who now are, and to those who shall be hereafter; in return for which the gods have given to them a well-
20 established kingdom, and will give them all other good things for
   ever;
   [may it be] with good fortune.

   It seemed fit to the priests throughout the country, to increase

majesty plundered *the* fields *of* other lands, *and* foreign countries to *the* conspicuous glory *and* prosperity *of the* country; *he* gave them to *the* palaces of *the* temples which had been plundered,

7 having made to spring up good fortune *and* joy *to* Egypt *with* rejoicing and praises; he fought *and* made war on behalf of *the* burial-places *against* the hated ones and *the* countries *of the* numerous barbarians, *he* cut off *the* heads *of the* barbarians, *and* those who govern them, justice he upheld *to* all the living men *and* women of the country, and *of the* other lands *of the* men *and* women under *his* dominion;

8   When, behold, it came to pass upon a year that the Nile failed on *the* right day *of the* season, all *the* living men *and* women of *the* cities, those were struck down *by* the event, when, behold, *the* evil fortune that had happened,

Having read *of the* destruction once upon a time *of* happiness befallen *in the* times *of former* chief sovereigns, under *whom* it happened *by* accident *that the* Nile failed to Egypt in *the* day *of*

9 *the* season; and his majesty (*may he be* praised) *and his* sister, they fed those who burn incense *in* the Egyptian temples, and likewise *the* various cities *of* Egypt.

At the times appointed he remitted numerous *taxes on* corn, he gave thousands *of* necessaries *and* expenses for *the* good welfare *of the* men *and* women each, he brought wheat *to* Egypt from the

10 Syrians *of* * * * city, from *the* land of Caphtor [or Phenicia], from *the* foreign island of Cyprus, which *is* in * * * *the* great sea, *and* great countries; he gave numerous *pieces of* silver *and* leek-plants, *and* spelt-seed *for* the good fortune *of the* living men *and* women;

By a decree from *the* land of * * * *city* he gave fame without end *of his* benevolence for ever; likewise they will talk *of the* revenues among the hereafter men *and* women; and *for these* so many things a gift from *the* gods *of the* established high office of

11 ruler *of* Upper *and* Lower Egypt with children of his own, and poor people, with servants unto times for ever; *with* good fortune.

And because of such things, *the* priests belonging to *the*

21 the before existing honours in the temples unto King Ptolemy and
Queen Berenice, the gods Euergetæ, and to their parents the
22 brother-gods, and to their forefathers the gods Soteres; and that
the priests which are in each of the temples throughout the
country should be further named priests also of the gods Euer-
23 getæ; and that there should be written on all their decrees, and
that on the rings which they wear should be further engraved also,
the priesthood of the gods Euergetæ;

24   And that there should be further appointed unto the now existing
four tribes, out of the multitude of priests which are in each
25 temple, a fifth tribe, to be named that of the gods Euergetæ; and
whereas with good fortune it also happened that the birth of King
26 Ptolemy, the *son* of the brother-gods, took place on the fifth *day*
of Dius, which also has been the origin of much good to all men;
27 that into this tribe should be chosen those who had been made
priests since the first year, and those who should be added until
the month of Mesore in the ninth year, and their descendants for
28 ever; but that those who had been priests before, until the first
year, should remain likewise in those tribes in which they had
29 been before, and also that their descendants should from the
present time be distributed into the same tribes in which their
fathers were;

30   And instead of the twenty priestly senators, who are now year
by year chosen out of the hitherto existing four tribes, of whom
five are taken from each tribe, there shall be twenty-five priestly
31 senators, five others being further taken out of the fifth tribe
belonging to the gods Euergetæ; and that those of the fifth tribe
32 belonging to the gods Euergetæ shall partake of the holy things,
and of all the other things in the temples; and that its chief

country were led further to prepare other expenses *for* King
Ptolemy living *for* ever, beloved *by* Pthah, and Queen Berenice,
the gods Euergetæ, in the temples, and for *the* brother-gods, *their*
12 buried parents, likewise for *the* gods Soteres, *who have been* laid
aside, *and for* those *the ancestors* beyond ; *and that* the priests *of*
each of all *the* Egyptian temples, belonging to *the* cities *of* Egypt,
hereafter should in addition be named priests'of the gods Euergetæ. They should add the name of *the* priestly high offices *to
be* written, *and the* further priestly office of chief builder unto
the gods Euergetæ *on* the signet-ring *to be* made, *and* worn upon
the hands ;

13   Another tribe *of* priests *shall be* appointed in *the* temples hereafter, *to be* in addition to the four tribes of old, *on* that day *to be*
made into a fifth tribe, for *the* gods Euergetæ. *And* whereas there
once happened, with good fortune and good fortune, because *the*
birth *of* King Ptolemy, living *for* ever, beloved *by* Pthah, son of
the brother-gods, in *the month* Dius, upon *the* fifth day, made *on*
14 that day our good *and* great happiness unto all *the* living men *and*
women ; *there shall be* enrolled *such* priests *as have been* already *of
the rank of* Soten *in the* temples, since that first year of his
majesty, and likewise those shall be enrolled, those immediately
going to be of that rank until *the month of* Mesore, in *the* ninth
year, within that tribe ; likewise those born *of them* for ever.
But the priests each, *it is* decreed, who had been added before *the*
15 first year of old into *the* appointed tribes *into* which they had been
added in like manner as before, *and* those born after that time,
shall be further kept among the scribes *of the* tribes which *were*
of *their* fathers, among those which *had been* made.

Instead of *the* twenty priestly senators chosen yearly by *the*
year out of *the* four existing tribes, *consisting* of five scribes, which
16 *are* from within each tribe, *there shall be* twenty-five priestly
senators ; five scribes in addition being divided off from the fifth
tribe belonging to *the* gods Euergetæ. *And there shall* be given
to *the* appointed fifth scribe belonging to *the* gods Euergetæ, from
all those things hitherto made, *the* purifications in *the* temple and

33 shall be so in respect to those things in which he is over the other
four tribes;

And whereas in every month the festivals of the gods Euergetæ
are celebrated in the temples according to the former decree (the
34 fifth, the ninth, and the twenty-fifth), and festivals and assemblies
at the national expense are performed every year to the other great
35 gods, there shall be held every year an assembly at the national
expense in the temples and throughout the whole country to King
36 Ptolemy and Queen Berenice, the gods Euergetæ, on the day in
which the star of Isis rises *heliacally*, which is considered by the
holy scribes to be the new year.

37 This is kept now in *this* ninth year on the new moon day of the
month of Payni, in which month are kept the little *festival* of
38 Bubastis, and the great *festival* of Bubastis, and the gathering of
the fruits, and the rising of the river takes place. But if it
should happen that the *heliacal* rising of the star passes on to an-
39 other day, because of the four years, the assembly shall not *so* pass
on, but be képt on the new moon day of Payni, on which *day* it
40 was kept from the beginning in the year, and it shall be celebrated
during five days with the carrying of crowns, and sacrifices, and
libations, and the other things that are fit;

41 So that the seasons also may do what is fit in every way according to the present arrangement of the world, and that it may
not happen that some of the national festivals, which are held in
the winter, should be sometimes held in the summer, *in conse-*
42 *quence of* the star moving one day in four years, and that others

all other things done in *the* sanctuaries of *the* country; and *the* chief of *that* tribe, the royal high-priest, *shall be* remembered like *as when* included in *the* established four tribes.

17 Whereas *there was* ordered *to be* kept an assembly unto *the* gods Euergctæ in *the* temples, *which* has been celebrated every month, upon *the* fifth day, upon *the* ninth day, *and upon the* twenty-fifth day, according to *the* writing made at first, *there was* added, and *there* was celebrated an assembly unto *the* great gods; *and* a festival throughout the country suitably in *every* year; there shall be celebrated a conspicuous suitable festival unto King
18 Ptolemy, living *for* ever, beloved *by* Pthah, and Queen Berenice, *the* gods Euergetæ, throughout the two regions *in* every city *of* Egypt at *the* time *when* the day of the star of Isis shining is placed, *which is* named the new-year's day *by* the scribes of heavenly life.

It is celebrated in *this* ninth year *in the month of* Payni, with holding an assembly of *the* new-year's day unto Pasht, *and* a festival unto Pasht in that month, * * * because of which the season for the religious ceremonies of all the fruits *and* the
19 overflowing of the Nile is celebrated. Behold a decree is made; behold if it should happen by accident *that the* changing *of the* festival of *the* star *of* Isis *shall be* placed a day further, because of *the* fourth year, by nothing *shall the* religious ceremony of that day be kept *at a later time;* that assembly shall be celebrated conspicuously, being begun upon *the month* of Payni, the first day, *as* the celebration of the assembly was
20 kept by us in *this* ninth year. That assembly shall be celebrated during five days with persons bringing diadems, with corn, with other sacrifices *on* the altar, the like doings, and all other things shall be celebrated *which were* made at a former time conspicuously;

Behold if it is done, the seasons shall be in respect of every
21 thing like *the* former decree which *was about* the heavens, *and* that day of the Dog-star shall not have a turning about, that it shall happen to come to pass at any time, by *the* decree *that* the assemblies *should be* made to change in *the* country, *that* those

of those now held in the summer, should be held in the winter ir

43 the future seasons, as had formerly happened to come to pass
from the arrangement of the natural year remaining of three

44 hundred and sixty days and of the five days which were after
wards ordered to be added; from the first day the festival of the
gods Euergetæ being now carried forward, because of *the* fou

45 years, on to the five *days* added on before the new *civil* year; se
that all men may know how the former defect in the arrangemen

46 of the seasons, and of the *natural* year, and of the decrees abou
the whole disposition of the pole, happened to be amended and
made perfect by the gods Euergetæ;

47   And whereas a daughter had been born to King Ptolemy and
Queen Berenice, the gods Euergetæ, and was named Berenice, whe
was immediately proclaimed a queen; and it happened that this

48 maiden, as on a sudden, passed away into the eternal world, while
the priests who had come up to the king for the year were ye

49 remaining near him, who immediately celebrating a great grief
for what had happened, having thought it right, persuaded the

50 king and queen to consecrate the goddess with Osiris in the
temple of Canopus, which is not only among the principa
temples, but is also very much honoured by the king and by al
men throughout the country.

51   And the bringing up of the sacred barge of Osiris is made te
this temple yearly out of the temple in the Heracleium on the
twenty-ninth day of Chœac, while the priests of the course o

52 all the temples, complete the sacrifices upon the altars dedicate
by them for each temple of those which are of the first rank, ou

which are held in winter should be held in *the* summer in each
season, *from* the change of the festival of *the* star of Isis by one
day, because of *the* fourth year *as* decreed ; *and the* other assemblies, behold, those which are held belonging to the summer
throughout Egypt, we should hold in *the* winter in *the* coming
22 seasons, like what happened to come to pass of old in *the* chief
provinces, because of *this* event, if behold *the* arrangement of the
year *shall be* made with days three hundred *and* sixty, and five
additional peculiar days ordered to be added; to celebrate the
additional first day of *the* assembly unto *the* gods Euergetæ away
from that day, because of *the* fourth year, until *the* added five
days additional, *which were* added upon the new-year's day; *so
that it* may be made known *to* all men *and* women about this
23 former defect *in the* arrangement in respect of *the* civil years and
the natural year, and *the* commands which relate to the judgments
of amendment of *the* faults *of* the heavens *which* happened to
come to pass, behold, *it·is the* production, *the* adornment solely,
and the excellence *of* the gods Euergetæ.

Whereas when a daughter *was born* unto King Ptolemy, living
for ever, beloved *by* Pthah, and Queen Berenice, *the* gods Euergetæ,
unto them, Berenice *was* her name, *she was* immediately pro-
24 claimed a queen; by accident, behold, the same goddess, a little
woman, *was* taken away into heaven, whilst *the* priests *who had*
come *from the* country near *the* king's presence, *were yet* remaining in *the* presence *of* his majesty, celebrating the great lamentation *and* the praises, considering about *the* particulars, they asked
from *the* king and queen, the gift from them, *to* grant *to* con-
25 secrate the same goddess like Osiris, in *the* temple of Canopus,
which *is* among *the* principal temples, for which great expense of
the Egyptians, expense for them *was* prepared by *the* king and *the*
living men *and* women of *the* country.

At *the* time *when*, behold, we shall draw along Osiris during *the*
drawing along *of the* barge to the same temple, at *the* season of
26 *the* year, from *the* temple which *is in* Heracleium, on the twenty-
ninth of *the month of* Chœac, *when* the Egyptians, *of the* principal temples at *the* time *of* completing *the* sacrifices *upon* the altars

c

53 of both the two divisions of the course, and with these things
   that are lawful towards her deification and towards the release
   from the grief they bestowed liberally and carefully, as upon the
54 Apis and Mnevis, upon whom it is lawful to be done;

     It seemed fit to pay to Queen Berenice, who had been born to
55 the gods Euergetæ, immortal honours in all the temples throughout the country; and in the month of Tybi, when she entered
   among the gods, (in which month also the daughter of the Sun
   in the beginning changed her life,) whom her father having set
56 up named at one time his crown, at another time his eyesight, and
   they keep a feast and a water-procession to her in most of the
   temples of the first rank;

57   In this month in which her deification in the beginning took
   place, to make also to Queen Berenice, the daughter of the gods
   Euergetæ, in all the temples throughout the country in the month
58 of Tybi, a festival and a water-procession for four days from the
   seventeenth day in which the water-procession and the release
   from the grief was at first made for her;

59   And to complete for her a sacred image of gold and *precious*
   stones in each of the temples of first and of second rank, and to
60 consecrate it in the holy place; and the prophet with the priests
   who enter the sanctuary for the robing of the gods shall carry it
   in his arms, when the goings out, and the assemblies of the other
61 gods, take place, so that when seen by all it may be honoured
   and worshipped, being called *the statue* of Berenice, queen of
   maidens.

of *the* principal temples, *by* the one part and the other part of *the* family *of* those of that temple, *are* joining with harps and all *the* other religious ceremonies for *the* celebration *of the* dedication *of* her raising up *as* a goddess, there was made for her a libation to

27 heal *the* grief *of* her raising up, they prepared them with perseverance *and* care, as the ceremonies for the Apis bull *and* Mnevis bull are celebrated;

It was determined *that there should be* given, according to a command, immortal honours unto Queen Berenice, *the* daughter of *the* gods Euergetæ, in *the* temples of *the* country *at the* times at which once upon a time she was taken up among *the* gods, in

28 the *month of* Tybi, (*the* month *in which* Ra himself took up his own daughter to heaven, *and that* is celebrated;) who unto him was named *the* apple *of his* eye, and *the* asp *the ornament* of his head, the beloved of her father. *They shall* celebrate unto her an assembly with a water-procession in *the* sanctuaries in the greater part *of the* temples of the first rank;

in this month *when the* making a goddess of *the* queen is celebrated; in addition there shall be celebrated one assembly, there shall be made one water-procession unto Queen Berenice, the

29 daughter of *the* gods Euergetæ, in *the* temples of *the* two regions, in *the* times of *the* month Tybi, from *the* seventeenth day, *when* was kept her water-procession, *and* was made for her a libation to heal *the* grief for her, it was celebrated as on the first day, during four days;

To set up a sacred statue unto that goddess of gold *and* all

30 polished stones in *the* temples of the first rank, in *the* temples of the second rank, at *the* times *of* consecrating in the holy place; the priest, the prophet, *of the sacred* barge, *with the* other chosen priests *of the* great purifications, *and* those who sing praises to the gods, *and* those who robe the gods, he shall carry it in his two arms, *so that* it may be seen on *the* day of *the* carrying out, and *of the* assemblies of *the* god, in *the* times; whereby it may be seen by all men and women *that* worship *is* to be paid at once

31 unto *the* distinguished Berenice, *and* how *the* queen of women *is* carried out.

c 2

62   And a royal crown is to be placed on her statue, more excellent
      than that placed on the statues of her mother the Queen Berenice,
      of two ears of corn, between which shall be an asp-shaped crown,
63 and behind this a papyrus-shaped sceptre of the same height,
      such as the goddesses are accustomed to hold in their hands,
      around which also the tail of the crown [or asp] shall be twisted, so
64 that from the arrangement of the crown, the name of Berenice
      may be clearly shown, according to the character of the sacred
      writing.

      And when the Kikellia are held in the month of Chœac, before
65 the water-procession of Osiris, the maidens of the temples shall
      prepare another image of Berenice, the queen of maidens, unto
      which they shall in like manner perform a sacrifice and the other
66 rites which ought to be performed at that feast;

      And it shall be lawful according to this for the other maidens,
      who wish to perform rites unto the goddess, to sing hymns to her,
67 both under the above-named priestly maidens, and those who
      furnish necessaries to the gods, when they put the proper crowns
      upon the gods, unto whom they are appointed to be priestesses;
68   And when the early corn seed shall show itself, the holy
      maidens shall bring ears of corn to be placed upon the image of
69 the goddess, and the men and women shall sing to her day by
      day in the festivals and assemblies of the other gods the songs,
70 which hymns the sacred scribes, when they have written out,
      shall give to the master of the singing, and of which copies shall
      be written into the sacred books.

71   And when the food is given to the priests out of the temples,
      when they are brought out to the multitude, there shall be given
      to the daughters of the priests, out of the holy revenue from the
72 day that they are born, the food adjudged by the priestly senators,
      those of each of the temples, according to the word of the priests
73 of the revenue; and the bread given to the wives of the priests
      shall have a divine pattern, and be called the bread of Berenice.

Behold, *it is* decreed *that* the crown upon *that* sacred statue *shall be* not less ceremonial *than the* appointed crown *on the* statues of her mother *the* Queen Berenice; *it is* to be placed conspicuously with two ears of corn, *and* an asp *on* the back, and a sceptre of papyrus flowers, to be held up; the papyrus flowers, the crown and the asp, the same as *what is* customary in the two hands *of the* goddesses; *the* tail of the same asp *is to be* twisted

32 *on* that sceptre; by which arrangement between those ears of corn *may be* shown the name of Berenice in the characters of *the* scribes of heavenly life.

And during *the* days *of the* celebration of the Kikellia, in *the month of* Chœac, in addition to *the* water-procession *of* Osiris, *it shall be* granted unto *the* women, *the* wives of *the* priests, to prepare another statue of Berenice chief *of* women, *and* to

33 perform sacrifices and other things, *which* shall be celebrated upon *the* days of that assembly.

By this, it is decreed, behold, for other women who are willing, *that* they shall celebrate their own unto that goddess, *and* sing hymns *to* that goddess, behold, under chosen priestesses, *and* servant-priestesses *who* carry *the* things that are carried of *the* gods, *to whom* they are appointed for priestly women.

When, behold, the early corn has sprung up *and* is con-

34 spicuous, *the* priestesses of the first rank shall bring ears of corn *and* give *them* to *the* statue of the same goddess; *they shall* sing songs to her upon appointed times; these songs the men *and* women, *both* husbands *and* wives shall sing *in* places, and assemblies, *at the* carrying out of *the* gods, songs from among which a man of heavenly life *shall* give unto *the* chief learned man of the singers *to* write a copy *in* the books of heavenly life.

Because of this when the dedicated loaves are distributed to

35 *the* priests from out of the temples to *those* already of the family of *the* chief priest *of the* temple *of any* place, *there shall be* distributed presence bread unto *the* daughters of *the* chiefs of *the* priests, since *the* day of their birth was celebrated, from the sacred dedicated loaves of *the* gods out of *the* presence bread *marked with* a pattern, *as* adjudged by *the* priests *the* senators in

And he that has been appointed superior and chief priest, in
74 each of the temples, and the scribes of the temples, shall write
   this decree upon a tablet of stone or copper in letters sacred, and
75 Egyptian, and Greek ; and shall place it in the most conspicuous
   place in the temples of first, of second, and of third *rank*, so that
   the priests throughout the country may show to those who honour
76 the gods Euergetæ what is right.

the sanctuaries *of the* two regions, henceforth agreeably to *the* command of *the* priests *of the* dedicated loaves; *and the* loaves 36 which are given to *the* wives of *the* priests *shall be* marked *with* a pattern impressed upon *the* loaf, put thereon; and they are to be named *the* loaves of Berenice.

The same learned prophet of *the* place, *the* consecrated scribe *of the* senators, *the representatives* of all *the* temple-priests, the chief of the temple-yard priests, and *the* scribes of *the* temples, 37 *shall* carve the inscription *on* a tablet of stone *or* copper, in letters of heavenly life, letters for books, letters for *the* Greeks, to be set up *in* a conspicuous place for men *and* women in *the* temples of the first rank, temples *of the* second rank, temples *of the* third rank, *so that* sight of it may be given to all men *and* women *how* preparation is to be made, by the priests of the temples of the cities of Egypt, for *the* gods Euergetæ and *their* children; behold, *the* religious ceremonies for *the* doings.

————

ABBREVIATIONS IN THE FOLLOWING PAGES.

D.S. means the Determinative Sign, or figure of an object, following its name spelt with letters.

Voc. means the Author's Vocabulary, accompanying his work on "Egyptian Hieroglyphics."

EXPLANATION OF THE HIEROGLYPHICS.

Line 1.

1   The YEAR; BAI, T, followed by a ring, the Determinative
Sign for Time, which is used also in the words Month and Day.
The first character is the *palm branch*, in Coptic ฿๐เ ; the second,
T, may be the feminine article; and the D.S. thus distinguishes
two words which were spelt and sounded nearly alike. This is
the ฿тоҫ, or *civil year*, used in dates, as distinguished from
No. 7, 33, the ฿мฺฑฺฑฺтоҫ, or *natural year* of the seasons. Voc. 953.
That the D.S. is a picture of the sun is shown at No. 5, 22,
where it has the vowel following it, and is the word, ρห, *the sun*.
The word BAI, for *year*, is not known in Coptic; but see No. 5,
22 : ฿тฺฐฺฑฺฑฺฑฺฑฺ, where our character for BAI is the last syllable,
MPI. The character for T is the picture of a Hill, and gains its
force from тฺ฿ฺฐฺ, *a hill*. The Hebrew letter n may perhaps be a
rude copy of it; as it is called by its Egyptian name, Tau.

2   NINTH; nine strokes followed by the definite article T, which,
however, in Coptic, is prefixed, not postfixed, to the Cardinal
number to make an Ordinal.

3   In the month of APELLAIUS, the Macedonian month which,
began in the middle of November; A,P,A,L,A,A,O,S, followed by
the ring, the D.S. for time. Here we might learn the force of
four letters, if they were not otherwise known. The hawk, in
Coptic ฿ฺฐฺฐฺฑฺฑฺ, may, by careless pronunciation, by dropping the
last letter, have been called AO, and hence given its force to
the letter. In this way all the letters probably received their
force. They had probably all, at first, syllabic sounds, rather than
alphabetic; and we shall see that those characters in which two
consonants were clearly sounded never got into use as letters.

4   UPON the DAY; S,S,O; ฿฿ฺฐฺฑฺ *upon*; with the word *Day*
omitted, but represented by the D.S. for Time. See No. 3, 21,
and 13, 42.

5   SEVENTH; seven strokes, but with no letters to make the Cardinal number into an Ordinal, as in the word *Ninth*, No. 2.

6   TYBI; the Egyptian month, written not phonetically, by characters whose sound represented the word, but symbolically, expressive of the meaning. The names of the months seem to be the only hieroglyphical words so written. The first character means FIRST, the second HOUSE, see Nos. 2, 18; the third R, for **IPI**, *to do;* making together THE FIRST OF HOUSING, followed by the D.S. for Time. Voc. 981, 995.

7   SEVENTEEN; seven strokes, with the half ring for ten, as at No. 15, 24.

8   ACCORDING TO; N, the preposition **ѝ**, *of.* Voc. 1292. This character is the representation of water, of which the Egyptian name was, as we learn from Horapollo, *Noun.* Hence came, after several changes, both the form and name of the Hebrew letter Nun.

9   The EGYPTIANS; CH, O, plural, a shortened form of CH, M,O, **ХHMI**, *Egypt.* Voc. 775. See No. 8, 31, which is not so shortened. It seems to be used as an adjective to the following substantive. See also *Saviour—Gods.* No. 12, 2, for the force of the first letter.

10   COUNTRY; the line with three dots is TO, the next letter, E or I, making **ТОI**, *lands;* followed by T, the definite article, which in Coptic would be prefixed; and by the circular D.S. for a City or Country. Voc. 777.

11   In the REIGN; CH, R,B. In Coptic **ХШРI** is *Powerful,* which may well be part of our word; **ХШРП**, is *to strike,* which is not quite so suitable. The last letter B is from **БШ**, and represents a club, or short sceptre. See No. 2, 19, where this letter is again used.

12   SE, T; the twig is **ѲЄ**, *a plant.* This is the name of one of the four orders of Egyptian priests. Voc. 644. It is usually spelt SETEN. Voc. 648. It is in Herodotus written Sethon, as the title of an Egyptian general; Manetho writes it Sethos as a title of Rameses II. It was used more particularly for the king of Upper Egypt, as the following priestly title was for Lower Egypt.

Together they represent the Greek word *King*, meaning of Upper and Lower Egypt. See No. 8, 24.

13   NOU, T; the name of an order of priests, and a royal title belonging more particularly to Lower Egypt. Voc. 663.

14   PTOLEMY; P,T,O,L,M,A,A,S. The king's name, including some of his titles, is written within an oval ring with a flat end. This ring seems meant to represent an engraved signet-ring. As the artist could not write the name on the flat seal, he has written it within the ring. The other royal names, as Arsinoe, Alexander, Berenice, are inclosed in the same ovals. The M in this name may be the origin of the Hebrew ם.

15   LIVING; here written with an O, the short for ONϩ Voc. 1402, 1407. This particular O, is never used except in this word. It may be seen carried in the hand of the Egyptian gods, and otherwise used as an ornament. It has been called a key; but the character for a key is drawn rather differently.

16   For EVER; H,T,N; ϩⲎ́ⲦⲈⲚ, *the end*, is the Coptic word nearest to this well-known hieroglyphic. Voc. 594. We may compare this with the Greek expression, in the New Testament, εις του αιωνα *until the* end of *the age*, or *until* the beginning of *the* next *age;* which we sometimes render *For ever*. The horizontal line is N, and is in place of the wavy line No. 1, 8, and must not be confounded with the T, the first letter in No. 1, 10. See the Rosetta stone, where this word is sometimes written with one form of N, and sometimes with the other.

17   By PTHAH, the god of Memphis, as Ra was of Thebes; P,T,H. Voc. 195.

18   BELOVED; M, for ⲙ̄ⲎⲒ *to love*. Voc. 1500. Together these two words mean *By Pthah beloved*. Had the word *Love* stood first, they would have meant *Loving Pthah*. Both forms were used by Rameses II., namely *Mi-amun*, and *Amun-mai*.

19   SON; S,E, for ⲱⲎⲢⲈ. Voc. 1789. The goose has the force of an S from ϭⲈ ⲩ̄Ⲉ, *a goose*.

20   OF; N, the proposition n̄; see No. 8.

21   PTOLEMY; see No. 1, 14.

22   ARSINOE; A,R,S,I,N,A, with T,S; of which S is the feminine

termination, and T the feminine article, which is prefixed in
Coptic, but in the Hieroglyphics ·usually postfixed, as in No.
14, 14; and sometimes inserted before the last letter, as in No.
9, 35 and No. 23, 47. The R in this name is the same character
as the L in Ptolemy. The Egyptians rarely distinguished those
two letters. The egg may have the force of an S, from being a
goose's egg, and used for the goose ⲤⲈⲰⲈ, or it may be from
the word ⲤⲰⲞⲨϩⲓ, *an egg.*

23   Bʀᴏᴛʜᴇʀ-ɢᴏᴅs, the title of the second Ptolemy and his
second queen; in Greek *Brother-loving.* This queen was also his
sister. The third Ptolemy was not the son of this queen, but of
the first wife, and hence not in strictness the son of the Brother-
gods. The hatchet or mallet has the force of NOU, from ⲚⲞⲨⲦ
to bruise, and represents ⲚⲞⲨⲦⲈ *a god,* with or without an additional T. The other character is S, for ⲤⲞⲚ *a brother.* See
No. 2, 12 for *Brother.*

24   Pʀɪᴇsᴛ, represented pictorially by a man in the act of making
a libation to the gods. As the word is not spelt, its sound is
doubtful. It may be the hieroglyphical word OTHPH, *dedicated,* from ⲞⲨⲞⲦⲈϩ *to pour out* an offering.

25   Oꜰ; N; Ⲛ, *of;* another form of the preposition, No. 1, 8.
See Voc. 1295. It represents the crown peculiar to Lower
Egypt, and worn by the priests of the order Nout, No. 13. Its
name was probably ᴇIN, and hence it is the letter N. The word
ⲞⲨⲈⲚ, *shining,* explains the meaning of its name, as it was the
Holy Crown of Exodus xxix. 6, the Bright Plate of Exod.
xxviii. 36.

26   Aʟᴇxᴀɴᴅᴇʀ; A,L,K,S,A,A,N,T,R,S; or to the mouth might
be given the force of RO, from ⲢⲞ, *a mouth;* and thus we should
have the vowel required to make Alexandros. The Greek R takes
its name Rho from the Egyptian name of this character. The hand
is a T, from ⲦⲞⲦ, *a hand;* and the Hebrew letter Teth, which is
also a hand, is known to be borrowed from this by its keeping its
Egyptian name.

27   Dᴇᴄᴇᴀsᴇᴅ; M,O; ⲘⲞⲨ *to die.* The second letter is of
doubtful force; but the place of the word shows what is required.

See Voc. 1645, also 1640, for the more usual forms of this word which is of very frequent use after a person's name.

. 28   AND; A,H; ⲁⲟⲁ *and.* Voc. 1271. The arm is A, a force which perhaps may be found in ⲙⲁⲟⲉ a *cubit* measure, in which word the ⲙ may be a servile affix.

29   The BROTHER-GODS, the same as No. 1, 23.

30   AND, the same as No. 1, 28.

31   The GODS EUERGETÆ, or BENEFACTORS, the title of the now reigning sovereigns, the third Ptolemy and his queen. The smaller character may ⲱⲁⲩ, *benevolent, useful.* We shall find it with the force of SH at No. 5, 16 ; No. 16, 34, and No. 29, 32. It represents ⲱⲉ *a staff,* and thence takes its name. The Egyptians, whether kings or great landowners, usually hold in their hands a long staff, which rests on the ground, called in Hebrew the staff of inheritance, and also a short sceptre. The character in this word is probably the staff, with the place for the hand to grasp it near the top, while the character in No. 1, 11, is the short sceptre, with the place for the hand near the bottom.

32   APOLLONIDES ; A,P,O,L,A,N,I,T,S, followed by the figure of a man sitting on the ground, the usual D.S. after the name of a private person. It answers the purpose of the ring, the sign of a royal name. The letter I is written by a double A ; the hand, T, has also the force of D, a letter not known in Egyptian words.

Line 2.

1   THAT, or *who,* meaning *the son of,* agreeably to the Greek idiom, where the word *Son* is omitted. It is PH,N, or P,N. See No. 2, 7 for the force of the P. See No. 13, 14 and 13, 47, also No. 2, 15 and 3, 26, where the same word has a P of a different form. Voc. 1376. We may conjecture that it represents ⲡⲓ *the,* ⲛⲧ *who,* as in its present form it is not found in Coptic.

2   MOSCHION ; E,M,O,S,K,I,A,N ; followed by the usual D.S. for a man. We very frequently find in hieroglyphics a vowel omitted before the liquids M,N, and R, but here, in a very unusual way, we find a vowel unnecessarily prefixed. The translator, in his care to write the Greek name fully, writes EM for M. The owl,

M, is often the syllable MO, and hence amongst the various forms of the letter M is chosen because it is to be followed by an O. The unnecessary addition of the O shows the translator's careful exactness. Towards the end of the inscription, letters are more freely omitted.

3   AND; A,O; ⲀⲨⲰ.   In other places this group represents ⲞⲨ, the prefix for the indefinite article.

4   MENECRATEIA; E,M,A,N,A,K,R,A,T,A, followed by the D.S. of a woman sitting. Here, as in the name of Moschion, No. 2, 2, we have E M very unnecessarily written for M. The more common D.S. for a woman is a figure sitting with the knees on the ground, and holding a flower in her hand, see Voc. 1757. But throughout this inscription she is distinguished from a man only by an ornament on the head.

5   The DAUGHTER; T,S,T. The one T is the definite article feminine, the other the feminine termination of the noun. Voc. 1797. See the word SON, No. 1, 19.

6   OF; N, the preposition ⲛ, as No. 1, 8.

7   PHILAMMON; PH,I,L,A,M,A,N, with D.S. of a man. The last two letters may be said to be misplaced for the artist's convenience. But it is often difficult to know which of two letters is to be read first, as in the cases of No. 1, 28, and No. 20, 2. The owl has its force as M from ⲙⲀⲨ, *solitary*, and is in Coptic ⲔⲀⲔⲔⲀⲙⲀⲨ, *the solitary of the dark*. Philammon is a Greek translation of the name Mi-amun; they both mean *Loving the God Amun*, and are formed like Philosopher, a *lover of wisdom*. They may be contrasted with Amun-mai, and Theophilus, which contain the word *Beloved*, not *Loving*; and they are a proof that the Egyptians, like the Jews, taught the duty of loving their gods, which remark cannot be made upon the names of Greeks and Romans.

8   BEARER, a figure carrying a burden on the head, which when joined to the next word BASKET, becomes BASKET-BEARER. But in other cases this figure is the word CONSPICUOUS. See No. 37, 18, &c.

9   Of BASKET; T,N,A, with the D.S. of a basket; probably

ХАПO, *a basket*, as in consequence of the nation's use of gutturals, the T and Th are not only confounded with H, but often with G, Ch, and K. Thus Champsi, the name of the crocodile in Herodotus, is in hieroglyphics Themsi, Voc. 1861, and gives its name to Lake Temsi; ⲈⲐⲰⲨⳋ Ethiopia is in Hebrew Cush. From the same reason Nubia, named from ⲚⲞⲨⲂ *gold*, is in Hebrew Knub, and Kub.

10   FOR; N,E,M, ⲚⲈⳚ. The unusual character written across the owl is probably E; see No. 23, 11, for this word written with a more usual letter, and No. 23, 18, and 24, 35, for the force of this unusual letter.

11   ARSINOE. See No. 1, 22.

12   BROTHER; see No. 1, 23, where the   rst letter forms part of *Brother-gods*. The word is here S,N,E; ⲤⲰⲚ, *brother*, but with a final vowel, which in Coptic would make it *sister*. But in hieroglyphics this particular E is usually a masculine termination, as to *Son* No. 1, 19; to *Father* No. 4, 4. It probably, like our final E mute, did no more than lengthen the foregoing vowel. The wine-bottle N, is in the large sculptures represented as transparent, and as only half full; and makes it probable that the Egyptians had a name for wine like our own name, and the Latin *Vinum*, and the Hebrew ין, which would give its force to that bottle as an N. Voc. 1837.

13   LOVING; M; ⳘⲈϨⲒ, *to love*. The character is ⲈⳘⲈ, a *plow* or *hoe*, and thus gains its force. Here we see that it is not always from the first letter in the word that the character takes its force as a letter, but from that which is most important. Had not the Greeks translated these two words Philadelphus, or *Brother-loving*, it would be more natural to read, *By brother beloved*, as in the case of No. 1, 16, and 17, where the adjective also follows the noun, and is read *By Pthah beloved*. Voc. 1499.

14   On DAY; E; ⲈⲢⲞⲞⲨ, followed by a circle, the D.S. of time. In No. 1, 1, the same D.S. was used for Year, and in No. 1, 3, for Month. Voc. 1010. See *Day*, No. 13, 46.

15   THAT, THE SAME; P,N, perhaps formed from the article ⲠⲒ *the*; as No. 2, 1. It is a pronoun following the substantive,

and so used in No. 3, 26 and 15, 9; which places quite establish its meaning. Compare No. 13, 49, *Our.*

16   A WRITING; S,SII,O,I, with the D.S. of a roll of papyrus tied round with string; cϩⲁⲓ *to write.* Voc. 331. The sitting man is here simply the letter I; compare Voc. 1982 and 1983.

17   The CHIEFS; A,O,MR, plural; ⲁⲙⲣⲏⲩ, the title of *chief bakers* in the Book of Genesis. The first two letters are the indefinite article Oⲩ; see No. 34, 33, for the word in its more simple form. Voc. 1328.

18   Of the TEMPLES; M,E, plural. The M is for the syllable Amun, the name of the god; E is ⲏⲓ, *a house,* in the plural ⲏⲟⲩ *houses;* hence Amun-ei, *a temple, or house of Amun.* The word Memnonium is Mi-amun-ei, *the house of one loving Amun.* The letter E in this word resembles the ground plan of a house, and is often used as the D.S. for *Temple.* The Egyptian temples were of various ranks of holiness, and we shall find three ranks spoken of in this Decree. This word embraces them all, including those of the lower ranks, and hence perhaps the letter E must be understood as the ground plan of a courtyard, which was less holy than the building, as that was less holy than the inner cell. Voc. 498.

19   HIGH PRIESTS; NOU,B; ⲛⲟⲩⲏⲃ *a priest,* a word formed, not from ⲛⲟⲩⲧ, *god,* as might be supposed from the hieroglyphics, but from ⲛⲁ ⲟⲩⲁⲃ, *belonging to what is holy.* Hence while the hieroglyphic seems related to No. 1, 29, it is not so etymologically. Compare Voc. 298, 302. The word is repeated three times, instead of adding the three strokes for the plural. In this way the sculptor makes his work more ornamental. The club, as at No. 1, 11, gains its force from ⲃⲱ, *wood.* If, as is probable, the various words for *Priest,* though translated alike in the Greek, represent men of different rank, this word means the priests of higher rank, while No. 1, 24, the man making a libation, is of lower rank, or may be the more general word, including priests of several kinds. See No. 12, 27 and 28, for further proof that this title belongs to the priests of the highest rank.

20   GUARDIANS OF THE TEMPLES, if we may read the characters

figuratively, while we are not helped by the Coptic language, or the Greek translation. Anubis the jackal, is the servant of the gods, and is here lying on the roof of the temple.

21   PURIFIERS; the characters are a flame of fire and a vase of water. Voc. 361. Compare No. 16, 23, where the D.S. for water changes this word into *Libations*.

22 Perhaps THOSE WHO SING, or PRAISE; S,EM,R,?,U; ⲥⲙⲟⲩ, *praise*, and ⲣⲱ a mouth. The owl and arm are EM; the flower, a doubtful character may be an O, from ⲟⲩⲱⲓ *to cultivate*. A flower has that force at No. 32, 6. See No. 30, 13, for the same word.

Line 3.

1   HYMNS; the bird is the word ⲟⲩⲣⲟ *king*, the perch on which it stands is T, making together, ⲟⲩⲣⲟⲧ *a hymn*. The three dots are the plural sign. Compare No. 3, 18, *His majesty*.

2   Perhaps THOSE WHO ROBE THE GODS. The principal character is a collar to be placed on the statue. See No. 30, 15.

The latter characters in this word, SN and three dots, are a very common plural ending in Hieroglyphics, but they are not met with in Coptic. They may be ⲥⲛⲁⲩ *two*, which would be a very natural form in Hebrew, where the plural is understood to mean *Two*, but little suitable here where the plural has always three strokes, and where the dual is so frequently used, as in No. 1, 23 and 29 and 31. On the other hand, in other inscriptions this termination is sometimes, though less frequently, spelt, TN and three dots. See No. 27, 16. For this we might find a more natural origin in the pronoun TN, which we often find following a substantive, as at No. 24, 6. Or it may be the indefinite plural article ϩⲁⲛ, prefixed in Coptic, but in hieroglyphics, as usual, postfixed. In some few cases this plural termination is written with SM, as perhaps No. 18, 12, and 32, 3.

3   WRITERS OF THE SACRED BOOKS. This must be understood as one word, because the plural sign covers the whole of it. The characters are an inkstand or pallet, with a reed pen for *Writing*, No. 15, 13; *God*, No. 5, 15; a roll of papyrus tied with a string, and T,E, the end of the word, *Book*, and the D.S. of a man.

4   Prophet; R, CH; forming ιρι, *to do*, and ϫⲱ, *speech*. In so rendering we are supported by the Greek. See *Fame*, No. 10, 23.

5   Others; CH, T, O, plural; ⲕⲉⲧ, *other*. Voc. 1127. See also No. 5, 25, &c.

6   Divine; NOU, T, F, plural; ⲛⲟⲩⲧ, *god*. The final F is ϥ *he*, and here seems to make the substantive into an adjective.

7   Probably Having purified themselves. The men seem to be pouring holy water upon themselves.

8   Being assembled together; H, A, ?, T, N, ?; S, N, plural; formed from ⲑⲟⲩⲱⲧ, *to assemble*. If the lock of hair be ϥⲟι, *hair*, the next syllable may be ⲛⲉϥ, *a sailor*, meaning that they came down the Nile by boat.

9   Having come; A, M. The feet are put on to the first letter as figurative of motion; and it may be from ⲁⲙⲉ, *to come*. See No. 24, 14.

10   The two provinces. The dual form of this word very much restricts its meaning. See No. 18, 7.

11   Upper and Lower Egypt; the D.S. of the two countries, each distinguished by its peculiar crown. That of Upper Egypt, with a ball on the top, is in Exodus xxviii. 36, 37, called the Linen Mitre, and that of Lower Egypt, the Bright Plate of gold, which was put over the former. When so placed they together formed the double crown called Pschent.

12   And; A, O, ⲁⲩⲱ, as No. 2, 3; more probably ⲟⲩ, the indefinite article, as in No. 5, 22.

13   Dius, the Macedonian month; T, I, A, O, S. The letter D was not known in Egypt.

14   Fifth day; the circle, the D.S. of time, for the word *Day*, and five strokes, the numeral.

15   The celebration. See No. 21, 16, and 21, 36.

16   Anniversary. The palm-branch is the word *Year*, as in No. 1, 1. The dish is part of the word *Assembly*, meaning a *Festival*, No. 18, 32, &c.

17   Of; the preposition as at No. 1, 25.

18   His majesty, is a convenient rendering of this group. It

contains the hawk with the whip of Osiris, which bird must be distinguished from the vowel A, which we have already met with so frequently. It is the word OⲨⲣⲟ, *king*, and often the name Horus. The sceptre in front we have seen in the word *Reign* No. 1, 11. The perch, a T, may make it a feminine word, while the F, ϥ, beneath, is the pronoun *His*.

19   Possibly WAS CELEBRATED CONSPICUOUSLY; A,M; perhaps Ⲉⲗⲗⲓ, *to remember*, with the D.S. of a man placing a crown on his head, which in this inscription is used for the word *conspicuous*. See No. 28, 43, *Celebrated*, and No. 37, 18, *conspicuous*. In the Rosetta Stone this latter character means *To wear a crown*, and is also part of the word *Kingdom*.

20   LIKEWISE; H,N,A, ⲋⲓⲛⲁ. Voc. 1273.

21   UPON; S,S,O, ⲥⲁⲥⲁ; the same as No. 1, 4, but with another form of the O.

22   The TWENTY-FIFTH DAY; with the circle, the D.S. for *Day* and the numerals as in No. 1, 7, and 29, 12.

23   OF; M, ⲙ, the sign of the genitive case, or the preposition See No. 6, 26.

24   MONTU, being a moon followed by SO, T,T, perhaps ϣⲱⲃⲧ *to change*, and the ring, the D.S. for time. The T,T, may stand for the Coptic ⲃⲧ, as the R,R, stands for ⲋⲣ in No. 10, 20 The star is very suitably chosen for an S in a word relating to the heavenly bodies.

25   THAT, THE SAME, as No. 2, 15. It follows its substantive. Voc. 1376.

26   RECEIVED; possibly ϣⲏⲡ, *to receive*, as the second character is a P. The first may be ϣⲏ, *wood*, meaning the wooden frame on which a weaver stretches his threads. The last is an A, and may be chosen symbolically, or it may be a D.S.

27   HIS MAJESTY, as No. 8, 18. It is the nominative case following the verb.

28   The KINGDOM; A, HOR, O; OⲨⲣⲟ, *king*; with a character the mark of an abstract idea. The bird is the royal bird, as in No. 3, 18, and 27. The last character corresponds to the Coptic prefix ⲙⲉⲧ, which changes OⲨⲣⲟ into ⲙⲉⲧOⲨⲣⲟ, *Kingdom*, and *Priest* into *Priesthood*, in the Rosetta Stone.

Line 4.

1 HIS, T,F; in the feminine, to agree with the word kingdom. T is a feminine article, as in No. 1, 22, and 2, 5, and elsewhere frequently. See No. 4, 5, for *His* in the masculine.

2 GREAT, CH, R,T, ϫⲱⲡⲓ, with the feminine article, as in the last word. Voc. 1603.

3 FROM; EM, ⲉⲙ; as No. 24, 35, where the vowel is of a different form. This is the same preposition as No. 3, 23, where it is written without the vowel. Voc. 1309.

4 FATHER; T,F,E; the word used on the Rosetta Stone. Voc. 1817. See No. 15, 17.

5 HIS. F, ⳽, the pronoun suffix. Compare No. 4, 1, where this pronoun is in the feminine.

6 HAVING CELEBRATED; A,M,O; possibly from ⲉⲙⲓ, *to remember*, as conjectured at No. 3, 19, and 19, 7.

7 RELIGIOUS HONOURS; T,O,T, with D.S, and S.N the plural termination of No. 3, 2, but without the three strokes. From ⲑⲟⲩⲱⲧ, *an image*, and also *a congregation.* See No. 17, 32, where the word is spelt rather differently, and No. 20, 22. Voc. 573.

8 IN or OF, R or L. There is no authority in Coptic for a preposition of this form, but this letter seems to have that force also on the Rosetta Stone, where we read very clearly "the blessings *of* a kingdom remaining to himself and his children." But in the Bashmuric dialect we have ⲉⲗ, the preposition *to*, borrowed perhaps from the Hebrew prefix, ל. Voc. 1335. Or it may be the common preposition ⲉϩⲣⲁⲓ, which elsewhere we find written RR.

9 TEMPLE, literally, DIVINE HOUSE, followed by T,E, ϩⲓ, *house*, with the feminine article. Thus the word is expressed first pictorially, and then by a letter, which letter is itself the ground plan of a house, or rather of a courtyard. Voc. 521.

10 OF; N,T; ⲛ̀ⲧ; the sign of the genitive. Voc. 1319.

11 GODS EUERGETÆ, as No. 1, 31.

12 WHICH; N,T,E, ⲛ̀ⲧⲉ. See No. 4, 10. The word is written in Coptic with or without the final vowel. In the Rosetta

Stone the preposition No. 4, 10, is spelt in this way. Voc. 1320.

13   IN; M; ελλ, the sign of the genitive. But in Hieroglyphics it seems to be a preposition with a very varying force of either *In*, *Of*, or *From*.

14   CANOPUS, so rendered in the Greek; P,K,O,T, followed by T, the feminine article, and then by the D.S. of a city. The city of Canopus is on the coast, about fifteen miles from Alexandria, and being at the mouth of the deepest branch of the Nile, it was rising in wealth and population with the growth of foreign trade; but when Alexander built his new capital, the trade of Canopus was stopped by an edict of Cleomenes, in favour of the Greeks of Alexandria. Canopus, however, remained a place of importance, and became the religious capital, and the centre of Egyptian learning. The priests had declared that the Canopic branch of the river, as being the deepest, was the Agathodæmian, or river-god. The jars with gods' heads, used in burial, were called Canopic jars. There Euergetes built a temple to Osiris, and the gold plate on which he dedicated to the god has lately been found. When Christianity rose in Alexandria in the second century, even the Greek paganism took refuge in Canopus. Eunapius and Rufinus, in the fourth century, testify to Canopus as being the seat of the ancient priestly learning, and of the study of hieroglyphics, together with the practice of a variety of magical and superstitious arts. All this very well agrees with its being the city in which the representatives of the Egyptian priesthood met in Senate in the reign of Ptolemy Euergetes.

15   DECLARED; I,R,H,T,R; ϼετοπ, *to urge*, which is from ετοπ, *force*, preceded by ιϼι, *to make*.

16   THIS; N,T, as No. 4, 10, and 4, 12.

17   DECREE; SOT, N; cottεn, *just*. The rabbit has its name from 6ωτϩ, *to burrow*; and its name, spelt SOAT, is written over a picture of the animal in Rosellini's "Monumenti Civile," pl. 20. This word is used so frequently on this tablet, that there can be no doubt about its meaning. Voc. 1692. See also the word cωτελλ, *to hear*. No. 31, 37.

18, 19   KING, as explained at No. 1, 12, and 13.

20   PTOLEMY; see No. 1, 14.

21, 22   LIVING FOR EVER; see No. 1, 15, and 16.

23, 24   BELOVED BY PTHAH; see No. 1, 17, and 18.

25   SON; see No. 1, 19.

26   OF; see No. 1, 8, and 20.

27   PTOLEMY; see No. 1, 21. .

28   AND; see No. 1, 28, and 30. In the former sentence the conjunction was omitted between No. 1, 21, and 22.

29   ARSINOE; see No. 1, 22.

30   The BROTHER-GODS; see No. 1, 23..

31   LIKEWISE; see No. 3, 20.

32   QUEEN; three letters followed by the D.S. of a woman, for which see No. 2, 4. Voc. 675. Without the final T, the feminine article, this word would have been *king*, No. 10, 43, Voc. 674.

33   BERENICE; B,R,N,I,K,A, with T,S, the feminine article and termination, as in No. 1, 22, and 4, 29.

34   His SISTER, or more literally, *Brother*, as the feminine termination is wanting. See No.8 , 40. Note, that Berenice was not the king's sister, but was so styled in compliment, as in Solomon's Song the king styles his wife his sister.

35   WIFE; E,T, followed by the D.S., a figure which in this case holds the ornament on her head. In Copic ϩⲁⲓ is *a husband*, to which if we add the feminine article T, we get this word *Wife*. Voc. 1833.

36   The GODS EUERGETÆ. See No. 1, 31.

37 . HE; P,E; ⲡⲏ; *He*, but meaning *They*; the singular used for the plural, as No. 24, 29. The Head, ⲁⲡⲉ, has the force of P.

38   MADE; I,R. from ⲓⲣⲓ, *to make*. See No. 17, 33; and also No. 16, 22, where the order of the letters is reversed.

39   COLUMNS; they are in the form of a papyrus stalk, with a bud for the capital.

Line 5.

1   EXPENSE; K,N, plural; ⲕⲏⲛ, *fruit, income*. This word bears

nearly the same meaning at No. 5, 40, and 9, 23, where it is followed by an arm, the D.S. of receiving.

2   GREAT, in the plural; see No. 4, 2, where it was in the feminine singular.

3   FOR; M, a preposition, used with similar force at No. 5, 32, though in the Coptic it is the sign of the genitive, meaning *of*.

4   The TEMPLES, as No. 2, 18.

5   OF; N,E, ℵⲁ, *belonging to*. See No. 1, 8, and 20, where it is spelt with an N only, and that of a different form; but see No. 11, 17, and 7, 22.   Voc. 1298.

6   COUNTRY; as No. 1, 10.

7   A,O; Oⲩ; the indefinite article, as at No. 6, 21, where it is equally not wanted.

8   EGYPT, in one of the very various ways in which it is written. The character above the figure of a country is at No. 17, 29, and No. 17, 35, very distinctly translated *At the public expense*, as of a festival.   At No. 21, 44, it is equally distinctly *Seasons* of the year.   In other inscriptions it is a *Sculptor*, being written over a man in that employment.   What it represents is doubtful.   But if we may give to it the force Chem, for ⲭⲏⲙⲓ, *Egypt*, in this place; it may then be part of Oⲩⲁⲃⲉⲙ, or *Suitable*, when applied to the festival; and ⲭⲓⲙⲓ, *to invent*, when the title of the artist. In what way it can mean the *Seasons* of the year is not clear.   In some such way we must try to reconcile seeming contradictions. See also No. 8, 9, where our difficulty about this character is further increased, and it has the force of Cham, but with another meaning.

9   ALL; the adjective belonging to *Temples*, No. 5, 4.   The basket or dish without a handle is NEB, and must be distinguished from the dish with a handle, which is K.   The final T is not found in the Coptic word ⲛⲓⲃⲓ, *all*, which this group represents.

10   HE; as No. 4, 37.

11   PREPARED; from CHⲃⲓ, *a sword*, which the two hands are holding, we get COⲃⲧⲉ, *to prepare*.   The final R is ⲓⲣⲓ, *to do*. See No. 25, 20, and 37, 34.

12   Possibly OBELISCS, or columns of another form from No. 4, 39.

13 Perhaps Colossal Statues ; P,P, plural, from ⲁϥⲱϥ, *a giant.* The Greek has only the general term *Honours,* in place of these more definite objects. See No. 4, 37, where the human head has the force of a P. At No. 27, 16, where this word is again rendered *Honours,* it can hardly mean colossal statues.

14 For ; the preposition, as No. 1, 8.

15 The Gods. Here the hatchet has the force of NOUT, and is followed by the vowel E, to make ⲛⲟⲩⲧⲉ. In Voc. 271 the word *God* is written with the hatchet and the letter T, giving to the hatchet the force of NOU. This particular final E is in hiero-glyphics very much confined to masculine words.

16 Probably Abundance; R, SH,A, ⲣⲉϣ; if we are right in giving to the second letter the force of SH, which we gave it in the name of Euergetes, No. 1, 31.

17 Great, the adjective following its substantive. See No. 5, 2, where this word was in the plural form, and No. 4, 2, where it was in the feminine.

18 Probably Necessaries, or *things fit;* SIOT, N ; ⲥⲟⲩⲧⲉⲛ, with S,N, the plural termination, as at No. 4, 7. The star may be ⲥⲓⲱⲧ, *the dog-star,* and the first two characters are inter-changeable with No. 4, 17. Voc. 1703. It is not usual for a sculptor to use such ornamental characters as the S,N, of this word for the unimportant grammatical termination. But it is frequent throughout this tablet.

19 Possibly When behold ; A,S,K ; ⲓⲥⲭⲉ, literally, *Behold if.* See No. 7, 30, and No, 20, 27.

20 He ; P,E ; ⲡⲏ ; the article for the pronoun, as No. 4, 37.

21 Possibly Supplied, or, according to the Greek, *Took care.* See No. 9, 3, where, with the addition of an R for ⲓⲣⲓ, *to do,* it may be rendered *Fed.* Possibly from the word ⲁϩⲱⲣ, *treasures, grain.*

22 Yearly; T,R,B,R,E, which is the Coptic word ⲉⲧⲉⲗⲁⲙⲡⲓ, or ⲉⲧⲉⲣⲟⲙⲡⲓ, the B being used for ⲙⲡ ; and followed by ⲣⲏ, *the sun,* which is no more than the D.S. for time of No. 1, 1. See No. 15, 27 for this word, and No. 15, 8, for ⲣⲏ, used for *Time.* With this use of B for MP we may compare that of

NT for D, in the case of Darius spelt NTARIUS. Here is well shown the uncertainty which hangs over the meaning of hieroglyphics when they are not followed by a D.S. In Egypt Incrip. pl. 28, is a procession of men, each carrying a palm-branch and the name of the branch is spelt with the first characters in this word yearly, T,R, for ΘⲰⲢⲒ, *a branch*, and the next character for its D.S. See Voc. 485.

23   ALL. See No. 5, 9, where this word has a final T. See also No. 29, 33.

24   THE ; as No. 5, 20.

25   OTHER THINGS ; as No. 3, 5.

26   THE BULL APIS ; H,A,P, followed by the D.S.

27   THE BULL MNEVIS ; E, for ⲈⳘⲈ, *a bull*, followed by CH, R, ⲬⲰⲢⲒ, *great*. Its more usual name, Muevis, is a Greek corruption of Amun-ehe. Voc. 65.

28   AND ; as No. 1, 28, and 30.

29   ANIMALS, is required by the Greek. The finger ⲦⲎⲂ, with E,O, plural, may be ⲦⲂⲚⲞⲞⲨⲈ, *an animal*.

30   TEMPLES, the building, with the word *God* upon it.

31   HE REGULATED ; it is so translated on the Rosetta Stone. Without the first character this is the word *Steersman*, written over the man in some sculptures. Voc. 1748 and 1746.

32   IN ; or FOR ; see No. 5, 3, and 6, 26.

33   CITIES ; B,K, ⲂⲀⲔⲒ, but without the D.S. or the sign of the plural ; as No. 18, 9.

34   EGYPT ; Voc. 798. From the eyebrow, and eyelids blackened with paint, according to the custom of the Egyptian ladies, we get the word ⲬⲀⲙⲈ, *black*, which represents ⲬⲎⲙⲒ, *Egypt*. The tear-drops may be caused from the pain which accompanies the operation of painting. The word is followed by the D.S. of a city, strictly speaking, but often used for a country.

35   GIFTS. The pyramid in the band is ⲦⲀⲨ, *a hill*, and represents ⲦⲎⲒ, *to give*, while the whole is symbolical of the act of giving. It is followed by S,N, the plural termination.

36   OTHER, or VARIOUS ; see No. 3, 5, and 5, 25. The adjective following its substantive.

37   GREAT, in the plural; the adjective following the substantive. See No. 5, 2.

38   Perhaps EXCELLENT; S,P,T, ϹΛΠΤ. If this is an adjective, it precedes its substantive.

39   GIFT. The hill ΤΛϤ, as held in the hand at No. 5, 35.

40   REVENUES may be the meaning of this word, which differs from No. 5, 1, in being followed by an arm, which is not in the act of giving, but is the same as that used in the words *Received*, No. 3, 26, and *Captured*, No. 6, 5.

Line 6.

1   AND; A,O, ΛⲰϤ, as No. 2, 3. These characters, at No. 5, 22, and often elsewhere, we read as OϤ, the indefinite article; but here, before a verb, that article would be out of place.

2   That he MIGHT MAKE; I,T, RO, ⲈⲐPO. The ⲈⲪ is the prefix of the subjunctive mood to the word ⲐⲢⲞ. The mouth ⲢⲞ, is either R, or RO.

3   RECONQUEST; E,M,K,R,O, plural, S,N; from ΧⲢⲞ, *to conquer*. The EM is the prefix of the noun's case. The SN is a very unnecessary second plural termination, or rather, should have been placed before the three dots. See No. 10, 29, and 10, 41, where we also have this peculiarity. Note the difference between the K in this word and the N in No. 6, 30.

4   SACRED IMAGES, so translated at No. 34, 3. It is formed of the hatchet for *Sacred*, see *God*, No. 5, 15; the systrum, the musical instrument used by the priestesses, and the D.S. of the statues.

5   CAPTURED; T,A,N, ΤⲰⲞϤⲚ, *to carry off*. The two legs are introduced to represent the action symbolically, see No. 6, 14; and the arm, the vowel, may have been chosen out of a variety of forms for the same reason; see No. 3, 26.

6   BARBARIANS, may be the meaning given to the rude figure here used as the D.S. The letters are A,S, ΛⱲⲈ, *a multitude*.

7   OF; as No. 5, 5.

8   PERSIA; P,R,S,T,T, with D.S. of land. See No. 6, 17, for the same D.S. See the same S in *Dius*, No. 3, 13.

9   He MADE WAR; R,R, MAS; ⲈⲢⲢHI, *to make war*, ⲘⲒⱲⲈ,

battle. The unfledged bird is ⲙⲗⲁⲥ, which gives us the sound required. See No. 7, 4. In this case the R,R, of the Hieroglyphics represent the Coptic ИR; as in Greek, where of the two R's the former carries the aspirate.

10   Possibly ON BEHALF OF. But this is doubtful. See, however, No. 7, 5, where we can give it the same meaning.

11   CITIES; as No. 5, 33.

12   EGYPT; as No. 5, 34.

13   With GOOD FORTUNE. See No. 6, 31, and 11, 10, where we safely give it this meaning. On the Rosetta Stone it is translated *Power;* Voc. 1451. But *Good fortune* will be seen to be its more literal rendering. It seems to be a compound character. The upright part may be T, see No. 13, 2; the lower part is an A; the line across it may be an O, see No. 13, 13; and the whole may be from ⲧⲁⲟⲩⲟ, *to send, to produce; to fall down, to cast down,* which approaches our word *Accident,* and *Fortune.*

14   Perhaps PLUNDERED, or perhaps *plundering;* A,T,N, from ⲓⲛⲓ, *to bring,* with T, the feminine article, as the nominative case to this verb ends with a T, and may very possibly be of the feminine gender. The form of the T may be chosen to represent motion.

15   HIS MAJESTY, as No. 3, 18, being the nominative to the foregoing verb. The first character we have seen as part of the word *Reign,* No. 1, 11. The bird is the word ⲟⲩⲣⲟ, *king.* The perch, T, makes it probable that the noun is feminine; it changes the word *King* into *Majesty;* and we see it in the more lengthened word ⲙⲛⲧⲉⲣⲟ, *kingdom,* which in Coptic is a feminine noun. The perch is chosen for a T, as a suitable character to accompany the bird.

16   Possibly, The FIELDS of OTHER LANDS. The first character is the moon, ⲓⲟⲋ; it may represent ⲓⲟⲋ,ⲓ, *the fields.* It is followed by TO, K,E; ⲑⲟ, *the world,* and ⲕⲉ, *foreign,* or *other.*

17   FOREIGN COUNTRIES. The first character is of doubtful force. It is the ornamental collar of No. 3, 2. If it is ⲙⲁⲓⲁⲕⲏ, *a collar,* it may be used to represent the two words ⲙⲁⲓ, *a place,* and ⲕⲉ, *foreign.* The last character is the usual D.S. for a country.

18   For or *unto*, as No. 1, 8, and 5, 14.

19   The Conspicuous glory. E,O, is ⲉⲟⲟⲩ, *glory;* the sitting figure, holding an ornament on the head, is translated *conspicuous* at No. 37, 18; the S which follows it is the sign of the feminine, prefixed in Coptic, but here postfixed to the adjective; and the plural sign treats the whole as one word.

20   The prosperity; N,N,F, with S plural, where we should look for S,N, plural; from ⲛⲁⲛⲉϥ, *good.*

21   Of the country, as No. 1, 10, and 5, 6, but preceded by the indefinite article, where the definite seems wanted, as Egypt is the country meant. See the article at No. 5, 22.

22   He gave; R,T,T. From ⲧⲏⲓ, *a gift,* with T the feminine article postfixed, and preceded by ⲓⲡⲓ, *to do,* which makes the substantive into a verb.

23   Them; N,F,S, plural, where as in No. 6, 20, we should have looked for S,N, plural. From ⲛⲁϥ, *to him,* made into *to them* by the plural signs.

24   Unto; R, a preposition as No. 4, 8; borrowed, as may be supposed, from the Hebrew.

25   Palaces, or houses with a throne; the throne, the letter T the feminine article, the D.S. for a house, and S,N, for the plural.

26   Of; M; ⲙ̄, the sign of the genitive case, as at No. 3, 23.

27   The Temples; as No. 2, 18.

28   Which had been robbed; M,N,M,N,T, with S,N, for the plural; from ⲙ̄ⲙⲟⲛⲧ, *not having.*

29   Perhaps, Who or they; A,M; ϩⲁⲛ, ϩⲉⲛ, or sometimes spelt ϩⲉⲙ, the plural article. See No. 15, 2, and 15, 36, where this word takes a plural termination, in the last of which places its meaning seems pretty well fixed by the Greek.

30   Having made to spring up, or *having added;* N,R; R, TE. From ⲡⲏⲧ, *to spring up,* preceded by ⲛⲉⲡⲉ, the prefix for the imperfect tense of the verb. See No. 14, 35, and 36, and No. 22, 18, where the verb has a different prefix. We must distinguish between our first letter, an N, and the K in the name of Berenice; though in several places in this inscription the distinction is lost, by the filling up of the hollow in the carving.

31   Good fortune, as No. 6, 13; but here preceded by S, as No. 10, 15; for which the reason is not obvious.

32   Joy; O,N,F; ογnoϥ.

33   Egypt; K,M, with T the feminine article, and the D.S. for a country. See No. 8, 31, and 32, where these letters, though of a different form, are used in the two words of the same meaning.

34   Probably, Rejoicing. The flower ℘ΔΗΔΙ may represent ογℨελλε, *a song.* The R may be ιρι, *to do,* which makes the substantive into a verb.

Line 7.

1   Praises; A,A,A,A; ΔΙΔΙ, *to magnify :* see No. 24, 28, where the word is in a more simple form; also Voc. 372 and 1449.

2   He; as No. 5, 10.

3   Fought; the two arms of a warrior, with sword and shield in his hands. Voc. 1777.

4   Made war; as No. 6, 9.

5   Perhaps, On behalf of, as conjectured at No. 6, 10. But here our unknown word has a plural termination, SM, instead of the more used SN. See No. 18, 12, and 32, 3, for other cases of such termination. The change between M and N if frequent. Our first letter does not seem to be the same as the S of No. 9, 21.

6   The burial places, literally, *Amenti,* the supposed place of the dead; A,M,N,T,T, with D.S. of country.

7   The; P, πε; see No. 5, 24, where, however, the P is followed by the vowel.

8   Hated ones; R,B,T; ℬⲱτε, *hated,* preceded by some part of the verb ιρι, *to do.* The second character is often used as a P, or B, in the word *Anubis;* Voc. 139.

9   And; see No. 1, 28.

10   Lands; the D.S. of No. 6, 17, repeated three times.

11   Barbarians; the D.S. of No. 6, 6. In these cases the sculptor shortens his work by omitting either the letter or the D.S. when the word occurs a second time.

12   Probably, Numerous; see No. 10, 8, where it will bear the

same meaning. A reptile from ⲱϫϯ, *to creep*, may give us the word ⲱϫ, *numerous*.

13   He cut off; T,R, from ⲦⲰⲢⲈ, *an axe*. But see No. 18, 8, where these letters mean ⲦⲎⲢ, *All.*

14   Heads; represented pictorially, and repeated three times for the plural.

15   The Barbarians; the D.S. as at No. 7, 11, followed by three dots, and S,N, the double plural termination. There are places in this inscription where these letters S,N, might be supposed to be the pronoun *Their;* but in such cases as this, and No. 8, 2, No. 9, 4, and others, such a meaning is unallowable.

16   Those who govern them, is required by the Greek, .CH, R,P,?,S,N, plural. The first two characters are ⲬⲰⲢⲒ, *powerful;* the fourth is doubtful.

17   Just laws; being the plural of No. 4, 17.

18   He; the article for the pronoun, as No. 7, 2.

19   Upheld, is required by the Greek, but the fourth character is doubtful. The word may perhaps be O,II,A; ⲟϧⲓ, *to uphold*, with the D.S. of a support of some kind.

20   The inhabitants, literally, the *living men* and *women;* the character for *Life;* see No. 1, 15, followed by the D.S. The woman is known from the man in this inscription by the ornament on her head; see No. 2, 4. Whenever throughout this decree the Greek writer wrote the word *Inhabitants*, or spoke of the people in general terms, the Egyptian scribe changed it into *Men and Women;* thus showing in the clearest way the higher rank that the women held in Egypt, compared with their sisters in Greece.

21   All; as at No. 5, 9, the adjective to the foregoing noun.

22   Of or *belonging to;* see No. 5, 5, and 11, 17.

23   The country, meaning, as it would seem, Egypt. But compare No. 6, 17.

24   And, as at No. 1, 30.

25   Other lands, as No. 6, 16.

26   Men and Women; the D.S. of No. 7, 20.

27   All, as No. 7, 21.

28　UNDER; M,N,II,I, CH,N, which seems to be compounded of the prepositions ⲙⲉⲛ, *with*, and ⲆⲀⲬⲉⲛ, *before*. Compare No. 32, 4 and 5.

29　DOMINION; the plural of the word rendered *Majesty* at No. 3, 18, and 27. Here, as might be expected, we have not got ⲧ the pronoun *His*.

30　BEHOLD, WHEN; as No. 5, 19.

31　IT CAME TO PASS; R,E,F; from ⲓⲡⲓ, *to do*, the auxiliary verb of action. REF is very exactly ⲉϥⲓⲡⲓ, *it was done*, with the pronoun F at the end of the word, as is usual in the hieroglyphics, not at the beginning, where it is placed in Coptic. See No. 13, 45, and 22, 5, where the same word is spelt rather differently.

32　UPON; H,R, ⲉⳅⲣⲀⲓ; as at No. 13, 22, and 24, 31. In other inscriptions these two letters are sometimes the name of the god Horus; see Voc. 119; and the first letter, when repeated, forms the word ⲐⲞ, *the world*, in the place of the second letter in our word No. 23, 37; see Voc. 705. Our preposition is derived from ⳅⲣⲀ, *the face*, which in Coptic forms part of a variety of prepositions, as do the words *Hand*, *Head*, and *Mouth*. The force of the letters is well proved when they occur joined with others; as No. 10, 33, ⲛⲀⳅⲣⲀ, *Hereafter*; No. 11, 38, and 12, 1 ⳅⲓⲡⲉⲛ, *For*; No. 15, 33, ⳅⲓⲡⲉⲙ, *Before*, and No. 12, 40, and 15, 40, ⲥⲀⳅⲡⲉ, *Upon, Within*. No. 8, 12, and 22, 3 can be better understood as *Event*, being the substantive ⳅⲣⲀ, ⲧ *face*.

33　YEAR, of the seasons; ενιαυτος, not ετος, *the civil* year, No. 1, 1 See No. 15, 29.

34　OF, see No. 1, 8, and 5, 14.

35　THE NILE; II,A,P, MO. The last syllable is ⲙⲟⲟⲨ, *water* HAP, though more usually IIAM, is a prefix by which ⲛⲟⲨⲃ *gold*, becomes ⳅⲀⲙⲛⲟⲨⲃ, and ⳅⲀⲛⲛⲟⲨⲃ, a *goldsmith*; ⳗⲉ *wood*, becomes ⳅⲀⲙⳗⲉ, a *carpenter*; so our word *Hap-mou* means a *Waterman*. Voc. 183. See No. 8, 29.

36　It FAILED; N,T,S, CH,M; ⲛ̀ⲧⲉ, the prefix of the verb, and ⲥⲀⲆⲉⲙ, *to fail*, or, as the Greek says, *to rise insufficiently*.

Line 8.

1   DAY; E,A,O; ⲉⲍⲟⲟⲩ. See No. 13, 13, where this word is written with two letters, and No. 13, 46, where it has only one letter; but the less careful spelling is supplied in those cases by the addition of the D.S.

2   SEASONS, or *times*. The meaning of this word is fixed very satisfactorily by No. 8, 23, and the first letter we treated as a P, or B, at No. 7, 8, and 23, 12. It may be AP *time*, a word which we find in ⲁⲡⲁⲥ, *old*, compounded of ⲁⲥ, *old;* and also in ⲁⲡⲣⲏⲧⲉ, *long ago*, compounded of ⲣⲏⲧ, *to rise*, or *raise*. It is followed by the ring, the D.S. of time, as at No. 1, 1, and 3; and then by S,N, the plural termination.

3   RIGHT; see No. 7, 17, *Justice;* and No. 4, 17, *Decree*.

4   THE INHABITANTS. See No. 7, 20.

5   ALL, the adjective following its substantive. See No. 7, 21.

6   OF, see No. 7, 22, and 5, 5.

7   CITIES; B,K; ⲃⲁⲕⲓ, with the usual D.S. Voc. 813. See No. 6, 11.

8   THOSE; N,E; ⲛⲓ, the plural definite article, followed by S,N, as the plural termination. See No. 20, 8, where we give a very different meaning to a similar word. But as the N is there a different character, it probably carried with it a different vowel's sound.

9   STRUCK DOWN. At No. 5, 8, we have seen reason for thinking this character has the force of CHEM. Here the Greek requires STRUCK DOWN, for which we find in Coptic ⲍⲟⲙⲍⲉⲙ, the half of which reduplicate word will very well satisfy our requirements, both as to sound and as to meaning, and particularly if we may join that half to the next word, and thus make a reduplicate word of our own. Such compound words are so far common in Coptic, as to make our conjecture not unreasonable.

10   CAST DOWN; N, CH; ⲛⲉⲝ.

11   THE. See No. 5, 24, and No. 9, 6.

12   EVENT, as No. 22, 3; H,R; ⲍⲣⲁ, *face*, a word used as part of the prepositions ⲉⲍⲣⲁ, *against*, and ⲛⲁⲍⲣⲁ, *upon*, and thus itself is the object towards which or from which motion is directed. See No. 7, 32, where the use of this word is explained.

13   WHEN BEHOLD, is the rendering that we gave to this word at No. 7, 30.

14   M, the prefix of the infinitive mood, to the next word. See No. 18, 20, and No. 18, 25.

15   The HAPPENING; S, CH,N. This word seems to be akin to CАϩЕМ, *to fail.* See No. 7, 36, where the characters are different, and it ends with M, not N. In many languages an *accident,* and *fortune,* are ambiguous words, and mean either good or bad. See No. 8, 27, and 13, 23 for other places where this word is used.

16   By FORTUNE, or *by accident.* This word is on the Rosetta Stone translated *Good fortune.* Voc. 157. It has the same ambiguity as the last word. See No. 13, 24. See also No. 30, 19, where this character bears its original meaning of *Two arms holding,* and where a possible explanation is offered for its secondary meaning in this place.

17   EVIL; CH, F,T,E; ϪⲰϥ; the adjective to the foregoing substantive. Compare No. 26, 20, *Avenger,* or *Next of kin.*

18   HAVING READ; S, SH,A,O; СϩАІ, *writing;* followed by a man with his hand to his mouth for the act of speaking, for the word ⲣⲰ, *mouth,* and then by S,N, to put the whole into the plural. We may compare this with the Hebrew, in which the word for *Reading,* means to *Read aloud,* namely, קרא, *to call out.* Our word means to speak the writing.

19   DESTRUCTIONS; CH, R,I, followed by D.S. of men thrown down. From ϪⲰⲣІ, *powerful.* With the adverb after it we have in Coptic, Ϫⲟⲣ ЕϬⲞⲖ, *destruction.* The D.S. makes the adverb less necessary.

20   Perhaps ONCE UPON A TIME; CH, P; ϪⲰⲠ, *hidden,* like the Hebrew עלם, *hidden,* which has the same two meanings as the Latin Olim, *formerly,* and *hereafter.* See No. 21, 6, and 21, 49, where it bears the same meaning.

21   HAPPINESS; ERO, T,T; ЕⲢⲞⲨⲞⲦ. See No. 13, 48, where it has the same meaning. The four jars have their force from their known contents, ЕⲣⲰⲦЕ, *milk;* and the T,T, seem not wanted. The second may be the feminine article. These jars form the first syllable of the well-known title of Osiris, Ro-t-amenti, *king*

of Amenti, which the Greeks wrote as Rhadamanthus. But see No. 25, 13, and No. 37, 24, where this same word is shown equally clearly to mean *principal* or *of first rank.* Such is the ambiguity attaching to this mode of writing, and which the scribes made no attempt to remove. The reason why they rested satisfied is pretty clear. They never meant to employ it on subjects requiring logical exactness.

22   BEFALLEN ; M,R,K ; from ⲣⲉⲕ, *to bow down,* with ⲗⲗ, the prefix of the infinitive mood ; as No. 8, 14.

23   TIME ; see No. 8, 2, where this word is in the plural.

24   KINGS OF UPPER EGYPT. See No. 1, 12, where we have the double title. The figure wears the crown of the Upper Province. See No. 3, 11. Very possibly the native sovereigns, the Kings of Thebes, are here more particularly pointed to.

25   CHIEFS ; A,P,A, with the plural sign ; ⲁⲡⲉ, *head.*

26   UPON ; as No. 7, 32, although the order of the letters is reversed. But in the case of H,R, with no vowel between them, the change of place of the two letters cannot be very important to the second. In the Greek we have εφ' ὦν, meaning *Under whom,* but here we have no pronoun. See No. 8, 12, where we render it *An event.*

27   IT HAPPENED. See No. 8, 15.

28   By FORTUNE, or ACCIDENT ; see No. 8, 16.

29   THE NILE ; see No. 7, 35.

30   FAILED, or ROSE INSUFFICIENTLY. See No. 7, 36, where this group ends with an M, not N, but is in every other respect written with the same characters. This connects the word No. 7, 36, with No. 8, 15, in which the characters employed are so different.

31, 32   THE EGYPTIANS, OF THE COUNTRY. See No. 1, 9, and 10, where these two words are thus united. Also Voc. 776.

33   IN ; M ; as No. 17, 3. See No. 5, 3, where a different form of the letter is used.

34   DAY ; as No. 8, 1, though it wants the final vowel.

35   SEASONS ; as No. 8, 2.

36   AND ; as No. 2, 3, and 6, 1.

E

37   His Majesty; as No. 3, 27.

38   May he be praised; H,S,F; ϩⲱⲥ, *to celebrate*, followed by
ϥ, in Coptic the prefix for the third person singular of the verb.
See the use of the ϥ at No. 13, 45.

39   And; see No. 1, 28.

40   Sister; S,N,E; literally *Brother*; for we must not compare
it to ⲥⲟⲛⲓ, *Sister*, for want of the feminine termination. See
No. 4, 34. The feminine termination is supplied by the D.S.

Line 9.

1   D.S. for the queen and king; the usual order of the two
being reversed. See No. 2, 4, for the D.S. of a woman.

2   He; the article used for the pronoun, as No. 5, 10. And
here, as there, the pronoun in the singular is used for the two
sovereigns.

3   Probably Fed; see No. 5, 21; where, however, we have
rendered these two words, *The food*.

4   Those; N,E, with S,N, for the plural. See No. 8, 8, where
this word is written with an N of a different form.

5   Who burn incense; M, SH, followed by the pot of incense
with a flame rising from it. The M is the prefix which makes
the verb into a participle. SH represents the compound word
ϣⲟⲩ ϣⲱⲟⲩ ϣⲓ, *to burn incense*. See the force of the SH at
No. 1, 31.

6   The, as No. 8, 11.

7   Egyptian, used as a plural adjective; see No. 1, 9, and 8, 31.

8   Temples, or *Divine houses*. The word *God* is used as an
adjective; see No. 12, 11; the D.S. for House, as at No. 28, 34,
is repeated three times.

9   Likewise; see No. 4, 31.

10   Various, or *Other*; CH, plural; ⲕⲟⲟⲩ. But see No. 1, 9,
where it is a contraction of ϧⲏⲗⲗⲓ, No. 8, 31.

11   Cities; as No. 5, 33.

12   Egypt; as No. 6, 12.

13   Probably Times. It may be the word ⲟⲩⲛⲱⲟⲩⲓ, *hours*.
See No. 12, 16, and 13, 7, which support this meaning to the
word. But the force of the third letter is uncertain.

14   APPOINTED; being the word translated *Just Laws* at No. 7, 17, but with different form of the S,N, the plural termination.

15   HE; the article for the pronoun, as No. 4, 37.

16   REMITTED; according to the Greek; S,A,?,O, followed by the man with hand to his mouth, RO, possibly some part of the auxiliary verb ΙΡΙ, *to do*. See No. 11, 40, and Voc. for this form of the S. It may be CΛϨΩ, *to make to cease*; but the force of the third letter is uncertain.

17   NUMEROUS, as No. 7, 12.

18   Probably SEED, meaning the tax on corn taken in kind; CH, A; ΧΟ, *seed*, or ΧΛ, *to sow*.

19   HE; as No. 9, 15.

20   GAVE; R,T,T; ╬ is one form of the verb ΤΗΙ, *to give*; the R is part of the auxiliary verb ΙΡΙ. The pyramid in the hand is the letter T, as No. 5, 39. Compare *Gifts*, No. 5, 35. The arm is symbolical of the action. This may also mean *He remitted.*

21   THOUSANDS, or HUNDREDS; S, with the plural termination S,N; ϢΗΕ, *a hundred*, or ϢΟ, *a thousand*.

22   Perhaps NECESSARIES. First we have A,O, the indefinite article ΟΥ; then H,T,R, ϨΤΟΡ, *necessary*. But the following characters, which form the word *Years*, and *Palm branches*, do not well agree with this. See No. 1, 1, *year*, and No. 5, 22, *yearly*, which both resemble this group of letters. The fruit of the palm tree was not so abundant, as likely to be here mentioned.

23   EXPENCES, as No. 5, 40.

24   FOR; the preposition, as No. 1, 8, and 13, 40.

25   The GOOD; N,E,N; ΝΛΝΕ.

26   WELFARE. The second character is *Life*, as No. 1, 15. The bird may be the fabulous phœnix.

27   Of MEN and WOMEN; the D.S. followed by three dots for the plural.

28   Probably EACH, or *singly*; A,O, with S,N, for the plural; perhaps ΟΥΛ, SINGLE. See No. 23, 20.

29   HE; the article for the pronoun, as No. 9, 2.

30   GAVE; being the same as No. 9, 20, but without the arm.

31   Probably WHEAT, agreeably to the Greek, more literally *Good*

E 2

corn; N,N,O, for ΝΑΝΟΥ, good; T perhaps the feminine article and the plow as the D.S. with the plural sign.

32 To EGYPT, as No. 6, 33, preceded by the indefinite article.

33 FROM; M, ⲙ, the sign of the genitive case, as 3, 23, and 5, 3

34 The SYRIANS, according to the Greek; R,T,N,N,O, with T,T and the D.S. for Land. The Rotenno are often mentioned in th inscriptions relating to the Egyptian wars.

35 Some unknown CITY, which may qualify the preceding word as it is not probable that whenever the Rotenno are mentione Syrians are meant. It was, perhaps, one of the ports on th Syrian coast. Our first letter is used at No. 26, 18, where it force is equally uncertain. The other letters are B,T,K, for ΒΑΚΙ *city*, with T the feminine article placed before the last letter o the word, as is not unusual.

36 FROM; as No. 9, 33.

37 The LAND; T,O, as at No. 6, 16, and the first part of No. 1, 10 though with a different form of the vowel.

38 OF; as No. 1, 8.

39 CAPHTOR, in the Greek, Phenicia. This was the land of th Philistines, called the Caphtorites in Deuteronomy ii.,23; but i is not the island of Caphtor spoken of in Jeremiah xlvii., 4, fror which the Philistines came forth, as also is said in Genesis x., 14 That was probably one of the large islands on the east side of th Delta, in the fork of two branches of the Nile. It is spelt K,F,T followed T,T, and the D.S. for a country.

40 FROM; as No. 9, 33, but with a different form of the M.

41 The FOREIGN ISLAND. The D.S. of an island is followed by th adjective K,E; ⲕⲉ foreign. See No. 6, 16.

42 OF; N,T; ⲛ̀ⲧⲉ. For the force of the two legs as T, se No. 10, 12; also No. 6, 28.

43 CYPRUS, according to the Greek; B,A,A,N,A,A; Βⲉⲛⲛⲉ *a palm tree*, in Greek Phœnix, whence its inhabitants, as also thos of the neighbouring country, were named Phenicians. The forc of the T,T, before the D.S. for *Land*, is doubtful. See No. 9, 34 and 39.

44 WHICH; NTE; ⲛ̀ⲧⲉ, ⲛ̀ⲧ, or ⲛⲉⲧ.

45　IN; the same preposition and character as No. 9, 40, there translated *From*.

46　The name, as it would seem, of the Mediterranean Sea. But the meaning is very doubtful.

Line 10.

1　The GREAT SEA; CH, probably for ⲭⲱⲡⲓ, *great*; and M, for ⲙⲱⲟⲩ, *water*. In Isaiah, xxiii., 3, the Mediterranean is called the Great Waters.

2　LIKEWISE, as No. 4, 31.

3　COUNTRIES; the D.S. of No. 9, 34, followed by T, and the plural sign.

4　GREAT; in the plural, to agree with the foregoing. See No. 5, 2.

5　HE; the article for the pronoun, as No. 4, 37, and 9, 29.

6　GAVE; as No. 9, 30.

7　SILVER VESSELS. The first character may be ⲑⲁⲧ, *silver*. The second is the D.S. In the Rosetta Stone, line 4, these two characters are united.

8　NUMEROUS, as No. 7, 12.

9　The indefinite article, as at No. 9, 22, and 9, 32.

10　The Greek does not help us to the meaning of this plural substantive, of which the first character is unknown.

11　LEEKS, the common food of the country; T,S, ISI; ⲧⲏⲥ, *a plant*, and ⲏⲟⲉ, *a leak*. The throne, in Coptic ⲑⲉⲙⲥⲓ, is softened into ISI, as we see in the name of the goddess Isis. The resemblance in sound, between the name of the goddess and the leek, made the leek a sacred plant. See Juvenal, who was told that Egyptians might not eat it:—

> Porrum et cepe nefas violare, ac frangere morsu.
> O sanctas gentes, quibus hæc nascuntur in hortis
> Numina.　　　　　　　　　　　　SAT. xv. 9—11.

12　SEED or *grain*; S,T, ⲥⲁⲧ, preceded by the indefinite article, ⲟⲩ.

13　SPELT; B,A,T, plural; ⲃⲱⲧ, *spelt*; or at least the grain mentioned in Exodus ix., 32, whatever its name may have been.

14　THE, the article, as No. 5, 24.

15　GOOD FORTUNE; as No. 6, 31. See No. 6, 13, and 11, 10, where this word has not the prefix S.

16 Of the INHABITANTS; as No. 7, 20; literally, *living men and women.*

17 DECREE; see No. 4, 17; but here the Greek does not help us, and there are four words to which we can give no exact meaning, except by supposing that they are out of place.

18 FROM; the preposition M, **ЛΛ**, as No. 9, 36.

19 The LAND, as No. 9, 37, and 7, 25.

20 Some CITY or *country*; but for this and the three preceding words we have nothing in the Greek.

21 HE; the article for the pronoun, as No. 10, 5.

22 GAVE; as No. 10, 6; but meaning, according to the Greek, *he left behind him.*

23 FAME; R, CH,O, with S,N, for the plural; **ХШ**, *to talk*, with the auxiliary **ΙΡΙ**, to act. See *Prophet*, or *Speaker*, No. 3, 4.

24 WITHOUT END; M,N, CH; **ⲁⲙⲛ̀ ХШ**.

25 Of BENEVOLENCE; being the word used in the king's name *Euergetes*, with S,N, for the plural. The letter is SH, for **ⲯⲁⲧ**, *benevolence.*

26 FOR or UNTO; R,R,E,A; **ⲉⲢⲢΗΙ**, *unto.* Here we have a double R, for HR, as in No. 6, 9, &c.

27 EVER; as No. 1, 16.

28 LIKEWISE; as No. 4, 31.

29 THEY WILL TALK; S,P, CH, three dots, and S,N, for the plural, perhaps from **ΠЄХЄ**, *to say*, preceded by S, which may be the future sign. In Coptic, **CNⲀ** is the prefix for the future, and we have no authority to treat S alone as such; but we shall see so many cases in this inscription in which it is so used, as quite to justify our so treating it.

30 REVENUES, or *expence*; as No. 5, 40.

31 AMONG, or *to*; as No. 4, 13, and 16, 31. But here, in the Vienna copy, the character is reversed, as it would seem, in mistake. It may be corrected by the help of Dr. Lepsius's copy.

32 THE, the article, as No. 5, 24, and 10, 14.

33 HEREAFTER, is required by the Greek; N,H,R, probably **NⲀⲢⲢⲀ**, *upon.* See No. 7, 32, for the force of the second letter, and an explanation of the word.

34   MEN AND WOMEN, as No. 7, 26.

35   AND, as No. 8, 39, &c.

36   So MANY THINGS; A,P,E,S, with S,N, for the plural; ANC, *a number*, and in the plural, *so many*. In the Greek we have, "In return for which."

37   A GIFT; see *Gave*, No. 10, 22, &c.

38   FROM; see *Of*, No. 1, 8, &c.

39   The GODS; as No. 5, 15. Such is the obscurity of this mode of writing, that we might have rendered this, "A gift to the gods," if the Greek had not cleared up the doubt.

40   ESTABLISHED; S,M,N,T; CⱭN̄T. See No. 13, 2, for the letter T. But also see No. 20, 39, where the same letters, varying only in the form of the S, must be read as SHALL NOT HAVE.

41   The HIGH OFFICE; A, HOR,O,?,T, three dots, and S,N, for the plural. The bird is not A, but HOR, as at No. 3, 27. The unknown character and the T represent the Coptic prefix, ⲘⲈⲐ, which is here postfixed. It makes a concrete noun into an abstract; as on the Rosetta Stone it makes *King* into *Kingdom*. Voc. 623; and *Priest* into *Priesthood*, Voc. 355. In Coptic, however, it precedes the word. Our word here may be ⲘⲈⲐⲞⲨⲢⲞ, and might be rendered *Kingship;* at No. 12, 27, it means an *Office* of a lower rank. The custom of giving the royal titles to the chief priest in every temple, had lowered the meaning of these titles.

42   OF; as No. 3, 17.

43   RULER or *King;* see *Queen*, No. 4, 32. As the second letter is K, we may conjecture that the first is HY; and then with the help of ⲰⲞⲞⲤ, *a shepherd*, we get Manetho's name for the Shepherd-kings, Hyk-sos. But the word HYK, for *King*, is not found in Coptic.

44   UPPER AND LOWER EGYPT, distinguished by two flowers; the lily for Upper Egypt shows several flower-leaves; the papyrus for Lower Egypt resembles a bell with a single-flower leaf.

45   WITH; as No. 3, 23, where it is rendered *of*.

46   CHILDREN. From the joint of *meat*, ϢⲠⲈ, we get ϢⲢⲞϮ, *children*, and ϢⲎⲠⲈ, *a son*. This character is used in the first

namc of this Ptolemy, and also in that of the next, for the word *Son*. Voc. 1806. See also No. 15, 21, for the use of this character.

Line 11.

1   Probably His own. N,O,O. The reed we have conjectured in Voc. 658, to have the force of OU, which would make this word ΝΟΥΟΥ, *his own;* as No. 33, 15. This reed, with a pair of leaves, should not be mistaken for the twig with four leaves, at No. 1, 12, which is an S. See also No. 26, 26, for the further use of this character.

2   AND; as No. 1, 28.

3   POOR PEOPLE, meaning, perhaps; *Labourers*, or *Dependants;* F,K,A,O,O, with S,N, for the plural; ϢΗΚΕ or ϢΩΚΕ, *poor.* The meaning is supported by the mention of *Servants*, in the same sentence.

4   WITH, as No. 10, 45.

5   SERVANTS; B,C,H, plural; ϦΩΚ, a *servant.*

6   UNTO, FOR; the preposition as No. 15, 37.

7   TIMES; R,?,O, with S,N for the plural. The meaning is very well proved at No. 12, 16, and 13, 7, and at No. 18, 12, and 25, 28, in which last two it is preceded by the same preposition.

8   FOR, or UNTO; as No. 10, 26.

9   EVER; as No. 10, 27, and 1, 16.

10   With GOOD FORTUNE; as No. 6, 13.

=

11   AND, as No. 11, 2.

12   Probably CONSIDERING; see No. 13, 28, where this meaning is also allowable. S,N,E,B, perhaps from ΝΙϦΕ *to inspire.*

13   The REASON; R,T,E; ΡΗΤΕ. See No. 29, 43, where it is the auxiliary verb. It must not be mistaken for *Give*, No. 9, 20, where the hand holds a pyramid.

14   Of SUCH THINGS; M,N,E, with S,N, for the plural. Or it might be taken as two words, M, the preposition *Of*, the other letters *These things*, as No. 9, 4, &c.

15   Perhaps THEY WERE LED, since, *It seemed fit to*, is what is required by the Greek; A,N; perhaps from ΕΝ, *to lead*, to

bring. The nominative case follows the verb. Or perhaps that thought may be included in the foregoing words; and then this may be the preposition *Unto*, as No. 32, 30.

16 The PRIESTS; as No. 1, 24.

17 OF, or BELONGING TO; as No. 5, 5.

18 The COUNTRY; as No. 1, 10, and 6, 21.

19 FURTHER; A,O,S, CH,R; CⲀⲪⲪHI, *from below;* preceded by the article Oⲣ. See No. 12, 7, and 12, 31, where it has nearly the same meaning.

20 To PREPARE; as No. 5, 11.

21 OTHER; as No. 5, 36, and 3, 5.

22 EXPENCES; as No. 5, 1. But here we have an additional N, where it would seem we want either S,N, for the plural, or nothing. See No. 11, 36, for a similar error in the artist.

23, 24, KING, as No. 1, 12, and 13.

25, 26, 27, 28. PTOLEMY, LIVING for EVER, BELOVED by PTHAH, as No. 1, 14, &c.

30 AND; as No. 1, 28, &c.

31 QUEEN; as No. 4, 32; but the word here ends with T,S, the feminine termination, as does the queen's name.

32 BERENICE; as No. 4, 33.

33 The GODS EUERGETÆ; as No. 1, 31, and 4, 36.

34 IN; as No. 5, 3, &c.

35 An uncertain word, perhaps, indeed, a faulty drawing in the Vienna copy. The first character Dr. Lepsius has, has an animal's head; then it becomes P,T; ⲠⲈⲦⲈ, *which,* or *the.*

36 TEMPLES; as No. 2, 18, &c., but here ending with S, and three dots, for the plural, in the same incorrect manner as No. 11, 22, where we had N, and three dots. In each case we ought to have S,N, and three dots.

37 AND; as No. 1, 28, &c.

38 FOR; H,R,N; ⳒⲒⲠⲈⲚ, as No. 12, 1, and No. 23, 28. See No. 7, 32, for an explanation of the first two letters.

39 The BROTHER GODS, as No. 1, 29, and 4, 30.

40 Their BURIED PARENTS; K,S,E,T, with S,N, for the plural; from KHC, *to bury,* and ⲒⲰⲦ, *father.* For the force of the S,

see No. 9, 16, and 34, 13. It is the first letter in the name of
queen Scemiophra.

41   LIKEWISE; as No. 4, 31, &c.

Line 12.

1   FOR; as No. 11, 38.

3   The SAVIOUR GODS, or GODS SOTERES. The adjective is CII,
𝐗; compare ΟΥΧΑΙ, *safety*, of which the first syllable is only
the article. See No. 1, 9; 8, 31, and 13, 2, for the force of
this letter.

4   LAID ASIDE; S, CH,E; ϹΚΗ.

5   Perhaps THOSE; the pronoun belonging to the foregoing
adjective. Voc. 1261.

6   THE; as No. 5, 24, &c.

7   Persons BEYOND; S, CH,R, with S,N, for the plural,
ϹΑϨΡΗΙ, *under* or *within*. See No. 20, 35, where it more
clearly means *former*.

8   PRIESTS; as No. 1, 24, &c.

9   EACH ONE; P,O; ΠΟΥΑ. The Greek has *Each of the
temples*. See No. 14, 33.

10   EGYPTIAN; as No. 8, 31, &c.

11   TEMPLES; as No. 9, 8; except that there the D.S. for *house*
is repeated three times.

12   ALL; as No. 8, 5, &c.; the adjective to the foregoing substantive.

13   OF; as No. 5, 5, &c.

14   CITIES; as No. 5, 33, and 6, 11, &c.

15   EGYPT; as No. 5, 34, and 6, 12, &c.

16   HEREAFTER, literally, TIMES, as No. 11, 7, &c.

17   IN ADDITION, *to add, to endeavour*; H,T,T; ϨΙ ΤΟΤ, *to
place the hand*, a word sometimes used as a verb, and sometimes,
as it would seem, as an adverb, *in addition*. See No. 13, 15
and 36, 9. As at No. 12, 39, the artist, in the choice of his
characters, takes one that is pictorially suitable.

18   The PRIESTS; as No. 1, 24, and 12, 8, &c.

19   OF; as No. 5, 5, and 12, 13, &c.

20   The GODS EUERGETÆ, as No. 1, 31, and 11, 33, &c.

21   THE, as No. 12, 6, &c.

22   NAMES. The ring within which a king's name is written, is used for the word, and is followed by S,N, for the plural.

23   Perhaps THEY ADD. The force of the first character is doubtful. But see No. 22, 17, and 36, where its meaning seems established.

24   THE; as No. 12, 21.

25   NAME; as No. 12, 22.

26   OF; as No. 1, 8, &c.

27   The HIGH OFFICE; as No. 10, 41. Literally, *The Kingship*, showing the ambitious nature of the title used by the high priests of the temples.

28   HIGH-PRIESTLY, the adjective in the plural, following its substantive. The hatchet is NOU, the character under it perhaps B; making ⲚⲞⲨⲎ́Ⲃ, *a priest*. Voc. 302 and 306. Compare *God*, No. 5, 15. The foregoing word tells us that among the various words for *Priest* which we find used in this Decree, that written by means of the hatchet, as No. 2, 19, describes those of highest rank.

29   To be WRITTEN. The character for writing is a pallette or inkstand, and a reed pen; it is followed by R, ⲓⲢⲓ, the auxiliary verb of action, and by S,N, for the plural. See *Scribe*, No. 15, 13, &c.

30   THE; as No. 12, 21, and 24.

31   FURTHER, or ADDITIONAL; S, CH,R,O; ⲤⲀⳘⲢⲎⲓ; as No. 20, 35. See No. 11, 19, and No. 12, 7, where the first three letters are of a different form, though of the same force.

32   OFFICE OF LORD OF THE BUILDERS; NEB, O, CH,T, followed by a tool, and the stone which the tool is to cut, as the D.S., and ending with the sign of abstraction, as at No. 12, 27, which makes *Lord* into *Lordship*. From ⲚⲎⲂ, *Lord*, and ⲈⲔⲰⲦ, *a builder*, and this from ⲔⲰⲦ, *to build*. This title seems to be that which Diodorus Siculus wrote Gnephachthus, as the name of an Egyptian king. As we see that it was a priestly office, it reminds us of the Roman priest's title of *Pontifex*, of which it may perhaps be the original.

33   PRIESTLY, as at No. 12, 28, the adjective following its substantive. See No. 2, 19.

34   UNTO or OF; as No. 1, 8, &c., but with an N of a different form.

35   The GODS EUERGETÆ; as No. 1, 31, &c.

36   THE; as No. 12, 24, &c.

37   SIGNET RING; CH, T,M, with the D.S. of the ring. This is the Hebrew word חתם, *to seal*, to which is allied the Coptic ϨⲒⲦⲉⲂⲤ, *to sign*. The seal is nearly the same in form as the ring for a name, No. 12, 22. Again, it is not very unlike the character for *Life*, No. 1, 15, and yet more like the character for a *Key*.

38   To BE MADE; A,R,E; ⲓⲣⲓ *to make*, with D.S. of the workman. See No. 16, 30.

39   For the HANDS; T,T; ⲦⲟⲦ, with S,N, for the plural. In choosing a letter T, the artist naturally takes one that assists his spelling. The hand, when held up, with the thumb away from the fingers, becomes the Hebrew letter *Teth*, ט, which, moreover, keeps its original Coptic name.

40   UPON, the preposition placed after its plural noun; or rather UPON THEM, the word *Them* meaning the *Hands*, the last word; S,H,R, ⲤⲀϨⲣⲉ, *within*, followed by S,N, the plural termination. See No. 22, 40, where ⲉϨⲣⲀ, the preposition in the same way follows its substantive. See also No. 7, 32, where this class of prepositions is explained.

41   Perhaps WORN; KI; ⲔⲎ *placed*. See No. 16, 43, and 19, 19.

1   A TRIBE, of Priests. See No. 13, 18, and 15, 31, where the recurrence of the word, with the required numerals, quite proves its meaning.

2   ANOTHER; CH, T; ⲔⲉⲦ as No. 30, 7. See No. 1, 9, and 8, 31, for the force of the CH; and No. 27, 15, for the force of the T.

3   PRIESTS, as No. 1, 24, &c.

4   Shall be APPOINTED. See No. 4, 17, and 8, 3.

5   IN; as No. 5, 3, &c.

6   The TEMPLES; as No. 2, 18, and 5, 4, &c.

7   HEREAFTER; as No. 12, 16.

8   IN ADDITION TO, seems here required, but the second letter is of

uncertain force. It is perhaps an H; and very probably the group is the same as No. 15, 21, the compound preposition ⲘⲘ and ⲈⲪⲢⲎⲒ, or rather in this case ⲘⲘ and ⲈⲢⲈ *also*. See No. 16, 6.

10 THE, as No. 12, 24, &c.

11 FOUR TRIBES; see No. 13, 1.

The four established orders of priests are shown on the Sarcophagus of Amyrtæus in the British Museum; see Egypt. Inscript. pl. 32. The first, the Soteno, wear the crown of Upper Egypt. Their name is nearly the same as No. 1, 12. The Nouto wear the crown of Lower Egypt; their name is No. 1, 13. The Othpho are those *dedicated;* their name is at No. 25, 1. The Bachano are the temple servants, and No. 33, 27 is probably one form of their names; but their name on the sarcophagus quoted is formed of the word No. 11, 5, *servants*.

12 Perhaps OF OLD; CH, P; ⲬⲰⲠ *to hide,* being the time lost sight of, as No. 8, 20, &c.

13 On DAY; A,O, the article; E,O, ⲈϨⲞⲞⲨ, day; R,E, ⲠⲎ the *sun,* used, perhaps, for the D.S. See No. 18, 14, where it has fewer letters.

14 THAT; the pronoun-adjective following the substantive; as No. 2, 15, and 3, 25.

15 To be MADE; H,T, O,T; ϨⲒ ⲦⲞⲦ, *to endeavour,* literally *to put out the hand.* See No. 12, 17.

16 INTO; the preposition, as No. 10, 42.

17 Probably *Conspicuous;* as No. 37, 18, where it is so rendered in the Greek.

18 FIFTH TRIBE; see No. 13, 1, and 16, 9.

19 FOR, or BELONGING TO; the preposition, as No. 1, 8, and No. 13, 16.

20 The GODS EUERGETÆ; as No. 1, 31, &c.

21 WHEREAS; R,N,T,E; R the preposition of No. 4, 8, and 15, 16; and ⲚⲦⲈ, ⲚⲦ, *which.* See No. 16, 45, where it has the same meaning.

22 UPON, as No. 7, 32; or EVENT, as No. 8, 12. We may read either, " When the *event* happened," or " *Upon* its happening." See No. 7, 32 for an explanation of this word.

23 It HAPPENED; as No. 8, 15, and 8, 27.

24   With FORTUNE; as No. 8, 16.

25   GOOD; the adjective following the substantive. The meaning of this character is very certain, from its use on the Rosetta Stone; but its sound is less so. It is probably a B, and represents ΟΥΑΒ, *holy*. Voc. 1387. See No. 14, 1.

26   AND, as No. 1, 28, &c.

27   Probably GOOD FORTUNE. See No. 6, 13, and 11, 10, where the character differs slightly from this.

28   CONSIDERING, is the meaning given to this word at No. 11, 12. It should be *Whereas*, according to the Greek, which tells us to alter the order of these last few words, thus: "Whereas it once happened with good fortune."

29   The BIRTH; M,S,T,O; from ΜΕC, *born*. The TO is like the plural suffix ΤΟΥ. See No. 35, 9, *Daughters*.

30, 31, KING; as No. 1, 12, and 13.

32, 33, 34, 35, 36, PTOLEMY, LIVING for EVER, BELOVED by PTHAH; as No. 1, 14—18.

37   SON; as No. 1, 19.

38   OF; as No. 1, 20, &c.

39   The BROTHER-GODS; as No. 1, 29.

40   IN, the preposition; as No. 13, 38, &c., with the usual irregularity in its meaning.

41   DIUS, the Macedonian month; as No. 3, 13, except that here it is followed, in mistake, by the D.S. of a city instead of the simple ring the D.S. of time.

42   UPON; as No. 1, 4, and 3, 21.

43   The FIFTH DAY; the numeral preceded by the D.S. for time without the word *Day*.

44   The indefinite article ΟΥ, prefixed to the following passive particle.

45   WHICH MADE; A,R,F, from ΙΡΕ, *to make*. The F postfixed is Ϥ, the prefix of an active verb, which thus becomes *He made*, or of its equivalent, the passive *It was made*, as No. 7, 31. See No. 8, 38, and 16, 39, for the Ϥ postfixed.

46   The DAY; as No. 2, 14.

47   THAT; the pronoun following its substantive; as No. 2, 1, and 14, 27, and with a different form of the P, No. 2, 15, and 3, 25.

48 HAPPINESS; EHO, T,E; as No. 8, 21, where it is followed by the feminine article.

49 OUR; P,O,N; ⲡⲱⲛ. This pronoun supports our reading PN as *That*; see No. 13, 47, and 2, 15, &c.

Line 14.

1 GOOD, the adjective following its substantive, *Happiness*. Of these characters the last, which, when alone, as at No. 13, 25, means *Good*, here seems like the D.S. to the preceding letters. These are I,B, and may be ⲟⲩⲁⲃ̇, *holy*.

2 GREAT, in the plural, as No. 5, 2, and 5, 37; another second adjective following its substantive, *Happiness*. But we see no reason for its being in the plural.

3 UNTO; as No. 10, 42; 13, 16; &c.

4 The LIVING MEN and WOMEN; as No. 8, 4, and 7, 20.

5 ALL; NEB,O; ⲛⲓⲃⲓ, *all*. Compare No. 5, 23, and 7, 21.

6 There shall be ENROLLED T,O,T; ϯϩⲓⲱⲧ, *to place*.

7 The PRIESTS; as No. 1, 24, &c. This, it will be observed, is a general word, including the priests of several, perhaps of all, ranks.

8 Probably ALREADY. See No. 14, 20, and 16, 21, and in particular No. 23, 45, where the Greek requires *Immediately*.

9 Of the rank of SOT, or SOTEN, as often spelt; S,T, with the D.S. of a man wearing the crown peculiar to that order of priests. See No. 1, 12.

Thus the new tribe is to be composed wholly of priests taken out of the highest tribe, that of the Soteno, giving thereby to the priests of that rank, as the governing body was elected by tribes, a double share of the representation.

10 TEMPLES; as No. 2, 18, &c., but preceded by the indefinite article ⲟⲩ.

11 FROM, or *since*, according to the Greek; literally, SH, A; ϣⲁ, *until*. But this difference is readily explained. This is only half the phrase, of which the latter half is No. 14, 21. Together they are ϣⲁ ⲙ̀ⲛⲁⲓ, *until this*; but when separated, with a date following each, the force of the two words rests on the second, and we must translate them *From—Until*. See No. 22, 28, and

33. This may be compared to the French Ne-pas, and Ne-point where, in consequence of the two words having been long used together, the meaning of the first is at last transferred on to the second. Our first character is a row of growing plants, and hence its force from ⲱϫⲉ, *a twig*. From this was copied the Hebrew letter *ɯ*.

12 THAT; as No. 3, 25, &c. It usually follows its substantive here it comes first, and is used for the article *The*.

13 YEAR; as No. 1, 1, being the civil year used in dates.

14 FIRST, in the feminine; as shown by the final T. See No 14, 39. No. 22, 23, is the same in the masculine. Perhap the T makes the Cardinal number into an Ordinal, as No. 1, 2

15 OF; as No. 1, 8, &c.

16 HIS MAJESTY; as No. 3, 18, and 27, &c.

17 LIKEWISE; as No. 4, 31, &c.

18 THOSE, though more literally THAT, in the singular; as No 9, 44; also No. 9, 42, with a different character for the second letter.

19 Shall be ENROLLED; T,O,T,O. See No. 14, 6, where this word is spelt with different characters; and also No. 4, 7, where th D.S. gives to these characters the meaning of *Religious Honours* and No. 17, 32; and 18, 25, where it means, *to be celebrated with* religious honours.

20 THOSE IMMEDIATELY; being the plural of No. 14, 8. Se No. 16, 21.

21 UNTIL, literally, M,N,O, ⲙⲛⲁⲓ, *this* or *hitherto*, preceded b the article. See No. 14, 11, where the two words ⲱϫⲁ ⲙⲛⲁ are explained.

22 The YEAR, being that used in dates; as No. 1, 1.

23 NINTH; the ordinal number, as No. 1, 2.

24 MESORE; the last month in the Egyptian year, pictured b four moons and water, meaning the fourth month of the season c inundation. As the inundation began about the 18th of July this month should begin on the 16th of October. But when th Calendar was adjusted, B.C. 1322, in the reign of Menophra, th months were already out of place, and this month then began o

the 13th of June, where, at the time, it was no doubt supposed it would remain. But in the course of years another change had taken place; and now, on the 9th year of Euergetes, the month of Mesore began about the 17th of September.

25   WITHIN; CH, R; €ⲐPHI. See No. 15, 7; 24, 16; and 35, 13, for this preposition.

26   TRIBE; as No. 13, 1, &c.

27   THAT; pronoun adjective following its substantive, as No. 13, 14, and 13, 47.

28   LIKEWISE; as No. 4, 31.

29   THOSE BORN; M,S,O, three dots, and S,N; ⲙⲉⲥ, *born*, with three plural terminations, the O for OⲨ, the dots, and S,N. See No. 15, 6; and also No. 13, 29 *Birth*.

30   FOR or UNTIL; as No. 10, 26, and 11, 8.

31   EVER; as No. 10, 27, and 11, 9.

32   The PRIESTS; as No. 1, 24, &c.

33   EACH; as No. 12, 9, though with an O of a different form.

34   It is DECREED; as No. 4, 17, &c.

35, 36   THOSE WHO HAD BEEN ADDED. No. 35 is N,R, the prefix ⲛⲉⲡⲉ of the past tense; and No. 36 is R,T,E; ⲡⲏⲧ, *grafted on.* See No. 6, 30, and 17, 18; also No. 15, 3.

37   BEFORE; R,M,N; for which we have in Coptic either ⲉⲣⲙ̄ or ⲉⲣⲛ̄.

38   The YEAR, as used in dates. See No. 1, 1.

39   FIRST; as No. 14, 14. It is in the feminine.

40   OF OLD; as No. 13, 12, and 16, 41.

41   IN; as No. 13, 5, &c.

42   The TRIBES; as No. 13, 11.

Line 15.

1   APPOINTED, in the plural; the adjective to the foregoing substantive. See *Decreed*, No. 14, 34.

2   Into WHICH; as No. 6, 29, and 15, 36.

3   THEY HAD BEEN ADDED; as No. 14, 35, and 36. Here the sculptor seems to have forgotten the prefix ⲛⲉⲡⲉ, and to have afterwards added a small N, to supply the want.

4   IN LIKE MANNER AS; II,T,T, from ϩⲉ, *like*. See No. 34, 38, where in the Greek it is rendered *A copy*.

5   BEFORE; R,R,R,N; ϩⲓⲡⲉⲛ, *before*. The RR are used for H,R, as at No. 10, 26; and the previous R may be also a preposition, as No. 11, 6, and 15, 37, making the whole a compound preposition in a manner not unusual.

6   THOSE BORN; as No. 14, 29.

7   AFTER; as required by the Greek. See No. 14, 25, where it is translated *Within*.

8   TIME, literally the SUN; R,E; ⲣⲏ. See No. 1, 1, &c., where the sun is the D.S. for Time; and No. 5, 22, where these two letters are so used.

9   THAT; the pronoun adjective to the foregoing substantive; as No. 3, 25, and 2, 15.

10   FURTHER; R,R,A; ⲉϩⲣⲏⲓ, the preposition; the RR for HR, as at No. 10, 26.

11   KEPT; II,R,H; ϩⲁⲣⲉϩ.

12   AMONG; the preposition, as No. 14, 41, &c.

13   The SCRIBES. The character represents a flat ruler, which is at the same time a pen-holder, and has several hollows for ink or paint; and to this is joined a reed pen. See No. 18, 22; also No. 37, 7, *Letters*, and No. 12, 29, *Written*.

14   The TRIBES; as No. 13, 1, preceded by the indefinite article ⲟⲩ.

15   WHICH; N,T,E; ⲛ̀ⲧ, as No. 9, 44, and 14, 18.

16   OF; the preposition, as No. 4, 8, &c.

17   FATHERS; T,F,E, with S,N, for the plural, as No. 4, 4.

18   AMONG; as No. 15, 12.

19   THOSE WHICH; P,T, with S,N, for the plural; ⲡⲉⲧ, *who*. See No. 16, 8; see also No. 4, 37, where the human head is a P, and No. 5, 13, where we have the head of another animal for that letter.

20   MADE; I,R,I; ⲓⲣⲓ, *to make*, as No. 17, 33.

=

21   INSTEAD, according to the Greek; a compound preposition; M, CHRE; ⲙ̀ and ⲉϩⲣⲏⲓ, *to, in*. From ϩⲣⲉ, *flesh*, we get the force of this joint of meat; as at No. 10, 46.

22   OF; as No. 3, 17, and 10, 42, &c.

23   PRIESTLY; the substantive used as an adjective.   See No. 1, 24, &c.

24   TWENTY; the numerals, as at No. 1, 7.

25   SENATORS, according to the Greek; ?, CH,T,O, plural; perhaps ΝΙϢϮ, a chief.   The first letter may be an N, in form a mallet, from ΝΕϩ, to bruise, and expressed oil.

26   CHOSEN, according to the Greek; M, followed by a character of doubtful force, and then by an R.   In the first name of Rameses II. this character is translated by Hermapion, Approved; "Approved by Ra."   We find it also in the name of Ptolemy Euergetes, where, by the help of the Rosetta Stone we read, "Approved by Pthah."   It is perhaps COTϭ, a scraping instru-ment; and thus may represent CETⲚ, to choose.

27   YEARLY; as No. 5, 22; T,R, BAI, for ΕΤΕΡΟϪⲚΙ.

28   BY or TO; as No. 1, 8, and 10, 38, and 13, 19, where we have very various meanings to this preposition.

29   YEAR; as No. 7, 83, being the year of the seasons, while at No. 15, 27, we had the civil year, as No. 1, 1.

30   OUT OF; M; ⲀⲖ, the preposition, as No. 5, 3, &c., where we have often translated it In.

32   The FOUR TRIBES, as No. 13, 1.   Here we learn that the ecclesiastical senate gave an equal weight to each of the four ranks of priests.   As the higher ranks consisted of a smaller number of priests, and yet had an equal number of represen-tative senators, they had a large share of the power.   And as the five new senators were all to be priests of the highest rank, that of the Soteno, these high priests gained by this Decree a still greater weight in the management of the ecclesiastical matters.

33   EXISTING, according to the Greek; perhaps Former; H,R,M, ϩΙⲡⲀⲖ, before.   See No. 7, 32, and also No. 11, 38.

34   SCRIBES; S,A, with D.S. of a man; CⲀϩ, to write or paint.

35   FIVE; the numerals; as No. 1, 7, &c.

36   WHO, or which; as No. 15, 2, but with a different M.

37   FROM, the preposition which we translated To, at No. 6, 24.

38   TRIBE; as No. 15, 32, &c.

39   EACH ; translated *First* at No. 14, 14.   There it had a final
T, the sign of the feminine.

40   WITHIN ; as No. 12, 40.   It follows its substantive as that
does, and would seem to make a compound preposition with
No. 15, 37.   See No. 7, 32, for the force of the letters.

41   PRIESTS ; as No. 14, 32, &c.

42   TWENTY-FIVE ; the numerals as No. 1, 7, and 15, 24.

Line 16.

1   An imperfect character or characters; perhaps P,E, ΠЄ the
article THE, as No. 8, 11, &c.

2   SENATORS, as No. 15, 25.

3   SCRIBES ; as No. 15, 34, but preceded by the indefinite
article, OⲨ.

4   FIVE ; the numerals, as No. 15, 35.

5   Perhaps DIVIDED OFF ; N,N,T,O ; ⲚⲀⲚ may be the plural
prefix, and ⲦOꞮ *to divide.*

6   IN ADDITION ; as No. 13, 8.   See also No. 22, 36, where the second
character, without the preposition M, clearly means *Additional.*

7   FROM ; as No. 15, 30.

8   THE ; P,T ; ΠЄⲦ, *who;* as No. 15, 19.

9   FIFTH TRIBE ; though there is no letter to make the cardinal
number into an ordinal.   See No. 15, 32, *Four tribes.*

10   BELONGING TO ; the preposition, or the prefix of the genitive
case, as No. 14, 3, &c.

11   The GODS EUERGETÆ ; as No. 1, 31, &c.

12   There shall BE GIVEN ; as No. 10, 22, &c.

13   A character of doubtful meaning, being the half of an oval ring
for a name, followed by N, *Unto.*

14   Perhaps The APPOINTED ; CH, O, plural ; ϪⲰ, *to appoint.*
See No. 1, 9, where this word is used as an abridgment of ϪΗⲘꞶ.

15   FIFTH TRIBE ; as No. 16, 9.

16   BELONGING TO ; as No. 16, 10.

17   The GODS EUERGETÆ ; as No. 16, 11, &c.

18   FROM ; as No. 15, 30, and 16, 7.

19   THOSE THINGS ; N,T,A, plural ; ⲚⲦ, ⲚⲦЄ.   See No. 15, 15,
where there is a different form of the vowel.

20 All; NEB, T,N; ⲛⲓⲃⲉⲛ, *all.* See No. 7, 27, and 16, 28, where we in the same way have a T more than is wanted for the word ⲛⲓⲃⲓ, *all.*

21 Hitherto; see No. 14, 8, where it is rendered *already*, and No. 14, 20; *immediately*.

22 Made; R,I; some part of the verb ⲓⲣⲓ *to make.* See No. 4, 38, where these characters are changed in their order. But as the verb begins and ends with an I, either letter may come first.

23 Purifications; as No. 2, 21; but here followed by the D.S. of water.

24 In; as No. 9, 45; but the same preposition as No. 16, 18, which is rendered *From.*

25 The temple, literally, *Divine building.* See No. 5, 30, *Temple*, and No. 2, 18, for *House.*

26 And; as No. 1, 28, &c.

27 Other things; as No. 5, 25, and 3, 5.

28 All; as No. 7, 27, &c.

29 The indefinite article, A,O; ⲟⲩ; as at No. 16, 3, &c. But from No. 20, 31, this would seem to be a part of the coming word.

30 Things done; A,R,E, with D.S. of the agent; and S,N, for the plural. See No. 12, 38.

31 In; as No. 4, 13, and 9, 40.

32 The sanctuaries; R, with E,A, for ⲎⲒ *house*, and the plural. The R is ⲣⲓ, a *cell*, or *room.* In the ecclesiastical writers it is the name of the hermits' cells. It here may mean the inner covered room in the temple, the Holy of Holies; and our compound word, with the article inserted between *Cell*, and *House*, becomes ⲉⲣⲫⲉⲓ, *the sanctuary of the temple.* See No. 28, 31.

33 Of the Country; the D.S. without the word. See No. 1, 10, &c.

34 The chief; SH, A; ϣⲉ, *a sceptre;* of which the first character is a picture. The Hebrew word for a Sceptre, often meaning a Tribe, should be rendered *Chief* in each of the following places: Genesis xlix., 16; 2 Sam. v., 1; and 2 Sam. vii., 7. See No. 1, 31, for this character.

35   OF; as No. 1, 8, &c.

36   The TRIBE; as No. 15, 38, &c. The D.S. of the man belongs in an unusual way, not to the word it follows, but to the word *Chief*, No. 16, 34.

37   Probably ROYAL, or some title for this chief priest. The bird may be either the letter A, as is more usual, or the syllable HOR for the god Horus, and ΟΥΡΟ, *king*. The difference between the two words is slightly shown in a careful sculpture, in the shorter neck, and more hooked beak, of the Royal bird; but if either the sculpture or the drawing is rude, this distinction is lost. The Royal bird is well distinguished at No. 3, 27, and 7, 29, by the whip of Osiris, which accompanies it. But the whip is absent from No. 6, 15, the same word. See No. 12, 27, where the office of high priest is called a *Kingship*.

38   HIGH PRIEST; as No. 2, 19.

39   Shall be REMEMBERED; A,M,F; ϵⲙⲙⲓ, *to remember*, with ⲥ the sign of the third person singular; as No. 19, 7.

40   LIKE; H; ϩⲉ, *like*; meaning perhaps *as when*. See No. 27, 6 where the H is followed by the vowel.

41   OF OLD, UPON A TIME, is the rendering that we have given to this word, at No. 13, 12, and 14, 40, &c.

42   IN; as No. 16, 18, &c.

43   ESTABLISHED; K,I; ⲕⲏ, *to place*. See No. 12, 41, and 19, 19.

44   FOUR TRIBES; as No. 15, 32.

=

45   WHEREAS, literally, UPON THIS; R, the preposition of No. 15 16, &c.; and N,T,E, ⲛ̇ⲧ, as No. 15, 15, and 9, 44.

46   THERE WAS; S,K,I; ϵⲥⲕⲏ, from ⲕⲏ, *to be*, with S the prefix of the feminine third person singular.

47   ORDERED, or *an order*; T,O; ⲧⲁⲩⲟ, *to tell*; as No. 22, 16.

48   To be KEPT; H,B; ϩⲱⲃ, *to make, to work, to use*.

49   An ASSEMBLY; as No. 18, 32, &c. The character may represent a boat with an awning over it; as the great Egyptian gatherings of people always took place by means of the Nile.

Line 17.

1   UNTO, or OF ; as No. 16, 10.

2   The GODS EUERGETÆ ; as No. 16, 11, &c.

3   IN ; as No. 8, 33.

4   THE TEMPLES ; as No. 2, 18, &c.

5   Perhaps, HAS BEEN CELEBRATED.   The dish, usually NEB, may be ꚍЄ҃Ӌ the prefix of the third person singular of the imperfect tense; the T,N, may be ꚍⲱⲟⲩⲛ, *to raise up, to magnify ;* they are followed by the sitting figure, the D.S. of a priest wearing ostrich feathers.

6· *Month ;* I,ℓ,T ; ЄⲂⲟꚍ, *a month ;* with R,E, ⲡ҃ⲏ *the sun* as the D.S. of time. The moon, ⲓⲟ𝔤, is I, or E ; the force of the star is doubtful. That, however, and the moon, are chosen for pictorial reasons, as much as for their force as letters.

7   EVERY, ALL ; as No. 16, 28, &c.

8   ON, IN ; as No. 16, 31, &c.

9   UPON, THE DAY ; S,S,O, with the D.S. of time; ⲥⲁⲥⲁ, *upon,* as No. 1, 4.   This preposition which here seems peculiar to dates, seems also unnecessary after the former.

10 FIFTH ; the cardinal number for the ordinal, as No. 16, 9.

11 UPON THE DAY ; as No. 17, 9.

12 NINTH ; the numeral, as No. 17, 10.

13 DAY TWENTY-FIFTH ; the D.S. for *Day,* the characters for *Ten,* as at No. 1, 7, &c., and the star with five points for *Five.*

14 ACCORDING TO ; the preposition, as No. 16, 18, &c.

15 MADE ; I,R, from ⲓⲡⲓ to make. See No. 4, 38.

16 WRITING, meaning *Decree ;* as No. 2, 16, but without the roll of papyrus there added as the D.S.

17 AT FIRST, or FROM THE BOTTOM ; S,H,H,A; ⲥⲁⳛⲡ҃ⲏ. Of the letters R,R, the first has the force of an H, or guttural, as in No. 6, 9, and 10, 26. The latter word is spelt with the same letters as this, excepting the S, with which this begins. See also No. 34, 26.

18 WAS ADDED ; as No. 14, 35, and 36.

19 AND ; A,O ; ⲁⲩⲱ ; as No. 2, 3 ; though these letters are more often the indefinite article ⲟⲩ.

20, 21   Was celebrated. No. 20 is the prefix ꞐⲈⲠⲈ as at No. 17, 18; No. 21, is I,O,T; to which we give the same meaning at No. 19, 40, and 21, 16. But perhaps No. 17, 19, which we have rendered *And*, as it is very properly rendered near the beginning of the Inscription, should here be considered as OꞭ, the prefix for the third person plural; and then our three words become one, and should be rendered *They celebrated*. We shall meet with this prefix to the verb at No. 19, 9, and No. 19, 19.

22   An assembly; as No. 16, 49.

23   Unto; as No. 16, 10.

24   The gods; as No. 5, 15.

25   Great; the adjective following its substantive, but without the plural sign. See No. 5, 2, &c.

26   A festival; so rendered in the Greek at No. 17, 34. See also No. 18, 37. The force of the first character is doubtful.

27   Throughout; so rendered in the Greek. At No. 19, 14, and No. 21, 10, we shall see a similar pictorial character used as the D.S. for *Turning about*. The R,M, may be, one or other of them, a preposition.

28   The country; as No. 1, 10, &c.

29   Possibly Suitable, an adjective belonging to *Festival*, No. 17, 26; A,O, CHEM,F; OꞭⲁⳢⲙⲉϥ, *what corresponds*, from OꞭⲁⳢⲉⲙ, *to answer*, to *renew*. See No. 5, 8, and 21, 44; also No. 8, 9, and No. 21, 51; all of which places present difficulties.

30   In; as No. 17, 1, &c.

31   A year, of the seasons; as No. 15, 29; meaning with its preposition, *Every year*. The scribe follows the Greek idiom, ϰατ' ενιαυτον.

32, 33   There is to be celebrated; M,T,O,T,O; from TOꞭⲰT, *a shrine*, with M, the prefix of the infinitive mood; and followed by I,R,E, ⲓⲣⲓ *to do*, the auxiliary verb, which makes the substantive into a verb. See No. 18, 25.

34   A festival, according to the Greek, as No. 18, 37. The first character is unknown, the last is SH, as at No. 1, 31, and 29, 32, and may be ⳤⲏⲁⲓ, *a festival*.

35   Perhaps Suitable; as No. 17, 29.

36   CONSPICUOUS; as No. 37, 18, where it is so translated in the
Greek; also No. 19, 34.

37   UNTO; as No. 17, 30, &c.

38, &c. KING PTOLEMY LIVING FOR EVER, BELOVED by PTHAH, AND
QUEEN BERENICE, the GODS EUERGETÆ; as No. 11, 23—33.

Line 18.

5   THROUGHOUT; M,N; 𝕷𝕴̄; At, in; as at No. 7, 28; or
N,M, 𝕹𝕰𝕷𝕷, At, as No. 23, 11, for the order of the letters is
doubtful.

6   THE; as No. 16, 8, &c.

7   TWO REGIONS, of Upper and Lower Egypt. The dual form of
the group proves its meaning, though there seems to be no difference between the two characters which should distinguish the
regions. See No. 3, 10.

8   EVERY; T,R; THP; as No. 36, 24.

9   CITY; B,K; ßΔKI; as No. 5, 33, and 6, 11.

10   Of EGYPT; as No. 9, 12, and 12, 15.

11   AT; the preposition as No. 6, 24, &c.

12   The TIME; as No. 11, 7, and 12, 16; here, however, the word
seems to end with SM, for the plural instead of SN, as is usual.
See 32, 3, for the same termination. Or, on the other hand, the
final letter may be wanting here, and the M may be a preposition.

13   OF; the preposition; as No. 16, 7, and 16, 18, &c.; unless
this letter be the termination of the last word. As the words
were written wholly by the ear, not spelt, as with us, according to
known laws, and not divided one from the other, it is highly
probable that the writer made the end of one word in part depend
upon the letter that followed it. Thus our word No. 18, 12, may
have lost its final N, because the next letter was an M.

14   The DAY; as No. 13, 46. See a longer form of the word
No. 13, 13.

15   SHINING, or appearing at the star's heliacal rising after it had
been for some days unseen before and after its conjunction with
the sun. This is the word *Illustrious* or *Epiphanes*, the title of
the fifth Ptolemy on the Rosetta Stone; except that there the E,

the first letter, is the same as the E in the foregoing word *Day ;*
thus, with the two legs, making the word more pictorial, as *Light-
bearing.*

16   Isis, according to the Greek ; being the word *God;* followed by
a pyramid for her name, and T,S, the feminine termination used
in the queens' names.   This name for the goddess is only used
in the case of her star, the Dog-star.   See No. 19, 17.

17   Star, represented pictorially.

18   Is placed; as No. 13, 15.   Or this might be taken as the
preposition ꙅᴀᴛᴏᴛ, *At, On,* a word the same etymologically.

19   The new year's day ; according to the Greek.   See No. 3, 16,
where it is rendered *Anniversary,* and means the king's birthday.

20   Named; being R,N, ᴘᴀɴ, *a name,* followed by F, the suffix
for *he* or *his,* and preceded by M, a prefix of a verb.

21   The; as No. 5, 24, &c.

22   Scribes; as No. 15, 13.

23   Of; as No. 8, 6, &c.

24   Heavenly life.   The first character is the arch of heaven, the
second is *Life,* as No. 1, 15, &c.   For these latter ·words the
Greek has *Sacred Scribes.*

=

25   It is celebrated.   See No. 17, 32, and 33, where this word
is compounded with the auxiliary ᴊᴘᴊ, *to do,* but without the final
F.   With that letter it is of the same grammatical form as No. 18,
20, *Named,* beginning with M for the infinitive mood, and ending
with F, which makes it a participle.

26   In ; as No. 15, 12, &c.

27   The year, that used in dates ; as No. 1, 1, and 14, 22, &c.

28   Ninth ; the cardinals for the numerals, as No. 16, 9, &c.

29   The month of Payni, described as the second month of the
season of inundation, by means of two moons, and the D.S. for
water, followed again by the word ᴘʜ, *the sun,* as the D.S. for time.
There are no hieroglyphical words so clearly symbolical as these
names of the months.   Other characters, while symbolical, or
pictorial to the eye, may very possibly have represented a sound ;
this name for a month represents not the letters of a name, but

its scientific description. Payni, in the Egyptian movable year, at this time began on the 19th of July, when the Dog-star rose. See the Calendar.

30   ON or WITH ; the preposition, as No. 18, 11.   Or this may be the auxiliary verb prefixed to the next word, as No. 21, 13.

31   The HOLDING, or CELEBRATING ; as No. 17, 21, and No. 19, 33.

32   An ASSEMBLY ; as No. 17, 22, &c.

33   OF ; as No. 17, 37, &c.

34   The NEW YEAR'S DAY ; as No. 18, 19, &c. ; but with a slight variation.   Compare No. 36, 6, *the pattern*, or mark, put upon the sacred loaves ; by which it would seem that this word is literally the *marked* day of *the year*.

35   UNTO ; as No. 17, 37, &c.

36   PASHT, the goddess of Bubastis ; her name followed by T,S, the feminine termination, as in the queens' names.   She is known on the monuments by having a cat's head.

37   FESTIVAL, called in the Greek the *great festival* ; as No. 17, 34.   Herodotus was present at one of these festivals in the City of Bubastis, and describes it in *lib.* II. 60.

38   UNTO ; as No. 18, 35.

39   PASHT ; as No. 18, 36, followed by the D.S. of a sitting figure.

40   IN ; the preposition, as No. 18, 26.

41   MONTH ; as No. 17, 6.

42   THAT, the pronoun adjective following its substantive ; as No. 13, 47, &c.

43   An unknown character, for which the Greek gives us no help.

44   BECAUSE OF ; as No. 16, 45, &c.

45   WHICH ; N,T,E ; ΝΕΤ ; as No. 15, 15, &c.

46   The SEASON ; as No. 17, 29, but in a shorter form.

47   FOR ; as No. 18, 33, &c.

Line 19.

1   RELIGIOUS CEREMONIES, as No, 4, 7.   But here we have an S, for which we can give no reason, except by supposing that the word should have ended with SN, for the plural, and that the sculptor remedied his omission by crowding in this S in a rather unsuitable place.

2   BECAUSE OF; the preposition; as No. 18, 44.

3   The FRUIT; T,O, plural; perhaps ⲞⲨⲦⲀⲈ, *fruit*, in which the first syllable may be only the article.

4   ALL; as No. 17, 7, &c.

5   The OVERFLOW; possibly ⲈⲞⲈⲒⲙ, *a flood*; but the force of the first character is uncertain.   The wavy lines may be D.S. for water, or may be in place of the final M in this word.   Horapollo says that the Egyptians call the Nile's inundation *Noun*, a word represented by these three characters for N.

6   The NILE; as No. 7, 35.

7   Is CELEBRATED, literally, *remembered*, as No. 3, 19, and 4, 6. Here, as at No. 16, 39, the word ends with F, the sign of the third person singular.

8   Possibly BEHOLD, the interjection; A,S; ⲒⲤ.   Compare ⲒⲤⲬⲈ *Behold if*, No. 19, 13; also No. 8, 13.

9   THEY MAKE; A,O, the prefix for the third person plural, ⲞⲨ A,R, ⲒⲢⲒ, *to make*; and F, the pronoun ⳓ of the third person singular.   See No. 16, 30.

10   A DECREE; as No. 4, 17, &c.

11   It HAPPENS; as No. 8, 15, &c.

12   By FORTUNE, or *accident*; as No. 8, 16, &c.

13   BEHOLD IF; as No. 8, 13, and 7, 30, where it is rendered *When*. We must here read, "If it happens by accident;" changing the order of the words as at No. 22, 7.

14   The CHANGING; SH, B; ⲱⲱⲂ, *to change*, with the serpentine line as D.S.   See the first letter in No. 36, 34.

15   The FESTIVAL; as No. 18, 37, &c.

16   OF; as No. 15, 28, &c.

17   ISIS, the name of the Dog-star; as No. 18, 16.

18   The STAR, represented pictorially; as No. 18, 17.

19   Shall be PLACED; from K,I, ⲔⲀ, *to place*, as No. 12, 4. More literally, *They shall place*, as it begins with A,O, the ⲞⲨ the sign of the third person plural, as at No. 19, 9.

20   A DAY; as No. 18, 14.

21   FURTHER ON; T,N,N,O; ⲦⲚⲚⲞⲞⲨ, *to send forward*.

22   BECAUSE OF, is required by the Greek ; but the meaning of the character is uncertain.

23   The YEAR, of the seasons, as No. 7, 33, and without the D.S. of the civil year, as No. 1, 1.

24   The FOURTH ; the numerals with the final T, which in Coptic changes the cardinal numbers into ordinals.

25   Probably BY NOTHING. The first letter, R, may be the preposition; the next two are the word *Not* in the speeches of the forty-two witnesses in the Book of the Dead; but here in the forms of a noun substantive with S,N, the plural termination. See *Not* at No. 31, 12.

26   The RELIGIOUS CEREMONIES ; T,O,T ; ⲐⲞⲨⲰⲦ, *an image ;* as No. 4, 7, and 19, 1.

27   The DAY ; as No. 19, 20, &c.   .

28   WAS MADE ; N,I,R ; ⲓⲡⲓ from *to make*, with ⲚⲈ the prefix of the past tense. See No. 20, 23, for the same word ; also No. 17, 33, for the verb without this prefix.

29   An ASSEMBLY ; being a compound word formed of No. 16, 48, *to keep*, and No. 16, 49, *an assembly*.

30   THAT ; the pronoun adjective following its substantive, as No. 14, 27, &c.

31   IT, the article for the pronoun ; as No. 5, 20, &c.

32   SHALL BE DONE ; S,R ; the auxiliary verb ⲓⲡⲓ *to do*, preceded by S, the sign of the future tense. Compare No. 31, 21, which is this and the next word united.

33   CELEBRATED ; as No. 17, 21, &c.

34   CONSPICUOUSLY ; as No. 17, 36, and No. 37, 18.

35   BEING BEGUN ; H,T,T,F ; ⲈⲓⲦⲞⲦ, *to begin*, followed by ⳓ the sign of third person singular, and preceded by the article ⲞⲨ. See No. 13, 15. This verb, meaning literally, *to place the hand*, has a variety of meanings, and often does little more than add emphasis.

36   UPON ; as No. 18, 40, &c.

37   The month Payni ; as No. 18, 29.

38   The DAY ; the D.S. for time, which here seems wanted for this word, rather than as part of the name of the month, as in No. 18, 29.

39 First ; as No. 14, 39, and 15, 39, in the former of which places it has a feminine termination.

40 The celebration ; as No. 19, 33 ; but here it is more convenient to use it as a substantive.

41 Of the Assembly ; as No. 18, 32, &c.

42 Was remembered, meaning, *was kept ;* as No. 29, 19.

43 Probably By us ; T,T,M ; ⲉⲧⲟⲧⲉⲛ with the hieroglyphic M in place of the Coptic N. The word ⲧⲟⲧ, *a hand,* forms part of many Coptic words as here, and in ϩⲓⲧⲟⲧ No. 19, 35. See No. 21, 41, where the writer also uses the first person plural.

44 The year, as used in dates. See No. 1, 1, &c.

Line 20.

1 Ninth ; as No. 1, 2.

2 Shall be celebrated ; as No. 19, 40, and 19, 33, and 18, 31 ; in all of which the order of the letters is more clearly shown than here. Here the T is understood to be below the bird, and therefore after it, in the same way that in No. 5, 15, *god ;* No. 10, 43, H,Y,K, *king ;* No. 1, 16, H,T,N, *ever ;* the upper letter is understood to be the first in the word. See, however, No. 16, 47, and No. 17, 32, where this rule is not followed, but the more natural one, that the character which comes first is to be read as the first.

3 An Assembly ; as No. 18, 32, &c.

4 That ; as No. 3, 25, and 19, 30, &c.

5 During ; the preposition, as No. 15, 37, &c.

6 Five days ; as No. 22, 14.

7 Diadem ; the upper part of the head tied with a ribband, which was the simple crown, or mark of royalty, worn by the Ptolemies, as is shown on their coins.

8 Persons bringing ; N,A, with S,N, for the plural ; ⲛⲁ *to bring.* But remark that we have here the same letters in the word *Those,* No. 8, 8.

9 With ; M, the preposition, as No. 25, 44 ; though the owl, the more ornamental form of the letter, is usually used, as No. 19, 36 ; 20, 11, &c.

10 Possibly Corn ; H,O, plural ; ϩⲟⲓ.

11 With ; as No. 20, 9 ; though with a different form of letter.

12   SACRIFICES, according to the Greek; M,S; ⲙⲁϣ, *to strike*, probably *to stay*.

13   OTHERS; as No. 3, 5, &c.

14   THE; as No. 18, 21, &c.

15   ALTAR; S,H,E,O; ϣϩⲟⲩ followed by the D.S. This is a basin standing on a pillar. The British Museum contains several such basins.

16   THE; as No. 20, 14, &c.

17   Perhaps DOINGS; I,R,O; from ⲓⲡⲓ with the plural termination ⲟⲩ. See No. 17, 33, and 15, 20, &c.

18   Perhaps SIMILAR; T,N,T, plural; from ⲧⲛ̀ⲧⲱⲛ, *similar*.

19   AND; as No. 16, 26, &c.

20   OTHER THINGS; as No. 20, 13, &c.

21   ALL; as No. 8, 5, &c.

22   SHALL BE CELEBRATED; as No. 4, 7; but here, as a verb with S, the prefix of the future tense, as No. 33, 1.

23   Which have been MADE; N,I,R, from ⲓⲡⲓ *to make*, with ⲛⲉ the prefix of the past tense. See No. 19, 28.

24   UNTIL; R,R,A; ⲉϩⲣⲏⲓ as No. 14, 30, &c. See the next word.

25   The EVENT; H,R, ϩⲣⲁ, *the face;* as No. 8, 12. This and the last word seem to make a compound word, meaning FORMERLY. See No. 7, 32, where this word is explained.

26   CONSPICUOUSLY; as No. 19, 34, &c.

═══

27   BEHOLD IF; A,S,K, the particle ⲓⲥⲭⲉ, which at No. 7, 30, means *When*, and at No. 19, 13, *If.*

28   IT IS DONE; R,T,R, some part of the auxiliary verb ⲓⲡⲓ *to make*. Compare No. 6, 2, which is spelt differently.

29   The SEASONS, ὡραι, according to the Greek; but the word is composed of the *civil years*, with a second plural termination. See No. 1, 1.

30   THE; as No. 20, 14, &c.

31   DOINGS; as No. 16, 29, and 30, with the same D.S., though spelt rather differently. See also No. 12, 38.

32   IN RESPECT OF, a compound preposition. The first R may be

the preposition, No. 18, 11, &c.; the R,R,I, ЄϨΡΗΙ *upon*, as No. 20, 24.

33   EVERY THING; CII, NEB,T. This is two words shortened into one. They are written in full at No. 16, 27, and 28. More nearly spelt like this is No. 26, 27.

34   LIKE; II,A; ϨЄ; as No. 16, 40, and 27, 6, and 21, 46.

35   FORMER; S, CII,R,O, plural; CAϪΡΗΙ, *beyond* or *beneath*. See No. 12, 7, where it means *Beyond*, backward into time, and therefore *Former*; and also No. 12, 31, where it is *Additional*.

36   DECREE or ARRANGEMENT; as No. 4, 17; 15, 1, &c.

37   WHICH, or THE; P,T; ΠЄΤЄ; as No. 16, 8, and 15, 19.

38   The HEAVENS; being P,T, the first the picture of the arch of heaven, and also ΠΗ, *the heavens*; the second the feminine article, which in Coptic is prefixed. The heavens are often represented by the goddess Neith, which is in agreement with the gender of the noun.

39   SHALL NOT HAVE; S,M,N,T; from ΙΙΙΙΟΝΤ, *not to have*, with S, the prefix of the future tense, of which we have seen so many examples. See No. 6, 28, *Not having*.

40   THE; as No. 20, 16, &c.

41   Possibly TURNING ABOUT; S,M; ϬЄΙΙЄ.

42   DAY; as No. 19, 27, &c.

Line 21.

1   THAT; the pronoun adjective following its substantive, as No. 3, 25, &c.

2   OF; as No. 15, 16, &c.

3   Probably THE WOLF; meaning the *Dog-star*; B,N,S; ΒШΝϢ. That the wolf gave its Egyptian name to the Dog-star appears probable from the word λυκαβας, *a year*, a word chiefly known in Alexandria, and which seems to mean the coming of the wolf.

4   Shall HAPPEN; as No. 19, 11, and 8, 15, &c., with S, the prefix of the future tense, as No. 20, 39.

5   To COME TO PASS, or BY FORTUNE; as No. 8, 16, and 19, 12, &c.

6   AT ANY TIME; as No. 14, 40, &c., where it means, *Of old*; here it means a future time.

7   BY; the preposition; as No. 21, 2, &c.

8   DECREE; as No. 4, 17; and 20, 36, &c.

9   The ASSEMBLIES; as No. 19, 41, &c.

10   MADE TO CHANGE; the pictorial figure of turning about, followed by R, for IPI the verb of action. See No. 21, 23, where this figure is the D.S. of change.

11   IN; as No. 19, 36, &c.

12   The COUNTRY; as No. 11, 18, &c.

13   THOSE WHICH ARE HELD; I,O,T. We have this word repeatedly so translated by the Greek. The R with which it begins is IPI, the auxiliary of action. See No. 19, 40.

14   IN; as No. 16, 31.

15   WINTER; according to the Greek. The year is divided into three seasons of Inundation, Housing, and Vegetation; and therefore no two words can correspond exactly with the summer and winter of the Greek. See the Egyptian Calendar.

16·   SHOULD BE HELD; as No. 21, 13. The difference in the characters, and the apparent difference in their order, does not alter the word.

17   IN; as No. 21, 14, but with an M of a different form.

18   SUMMER, or the season of inundation, marked by the character for water.

19   IN; as No. 21, 17, &c.

20   Perhaps SEASON, as No. 21, 44, and No. 25, 41; compare No. 5, 8, where the force of this character is explained.

21   EACH, as at No. 15, 39; though more often *First*, as No. 19, 39, or *One*, as No. 21, 29.

22   THE; as No. 20, 14, &c.

23   CHANGE; as No. 19, 14.

24   The FESTIVAL; as No. 19, 15.

25   OF; as No. 19, 16, &c.

26   The STAR OF ISIS; as No. 19, 17, and 18; but here the figure of the star is omitted.

27   BY; as No. 21, 17, &c.

28   DAY; as No. 20, 42, &c.

29   ONE; as No. 21, 21, &c.

30   BECAUSE OF; according to the Greek. This is a sitting figure,
holding the sacred whip of Osiris; and from the first syllable in
his name we have **ⲁ.ⲩ** or **ⲉ.ⲩ**, *why*. See No. 22, 31, where
we give it the same meaning.

31   The FOURTH YEAR. The final T makes the cardinal number
into an ordinal. This is the year of the seasons, as No. 19, 23,
and 24.

32   As DECREED. The R may be the verb of action **ⲓⲣⲓ**. See
DECREE, No. 20, 36, &c.; and No. 31, 14, where the same
auxiliary verb of action is employed.

33   OTHER; K,T, CH,T, plural; **ⲕⲉⲧ**, **ϫⲉⲧ**. Each of these
words means *Other;* they are here joined, making a reduplicate
word, in a form common in the Coptic language. The wish of
the sculptor to make his inscription ornamental is here shown by
his using the pyramid as one of the letters in this very unimportant word.

34   ASSEMBLIES; as No. 21, 9, &c.

35   BEHOLD. So we have ventured to render this at No. 19, 8, &c.

36   THOSE WHICH ARE HELD, as No. 21, 16.   But here we have
not got the verb of action.

37   BELONGING TO; as No. 1, 8.   But remark that No. 21, 14
the preposition holding the same place in a similar sentence, is an
M, not an N. But the Coptic language is equally irregular in
the use of its prepositions.

38   SUMMER; as No. 21, 18.

39   THROUGHOUT; E,M, the preposition **ⲛ̀**, as No. 21, 19. For
the force of the vowel, see No. 4, 35; and 34, 18.

40   EGYPT. See Voc. 790 and 792. The first character, when
drawn more carefully, is a crocodile's tail; and thus the word
Champsi, Herodotus's name for the crocodile, represents the word
ϫⲏⲙⲓ, *Egypt.*

41   WE SHALL HOLD; the word IOT, to which we have so often given
this meaning, preceded by T,N, the Coptic prefix **ⲧⲉⲛ** for the
first person plural of a verb. Remark that though the Greek does
not make the writer speak in the first person, yet the hieroglyphics
do, not only here, but at No. 19, 43.

42   IN; as No. 21, 37, &c.

43   WINTER; as No. 21, 15, but here in the plural.

44   In the SEASONS, according to the Greek; A,O, KEM, plural, possibly ⲞⲨⲀϨⲈⲘ, *a renewal.* See No. 5, 8, where we gave the force of CHEM to the peculiar character in this word; and also No. 17, 29, and 35, where we rendered this word as *Suitable;* also No. 25, 41, *Season.*

45   COMING; A, or rather I, with S,N, for the plural; from Ī, *to come.* See No. 3, 9. This letter with two legs is chosen in order to distinguish it as a verb relating to motion.

46   LIKE; as No. 20, 34.

47   What HAPPENED; as No. 19, 11, &c.

48   To COME TO PASS; as No. 19, 12, &c. Here the Greek is very exactly translated by these two words.

49   OF OLD; or ONCE UPON A TIME; as No. 21, 6.

50   IN; as No. 21, 14, &c.

51   Here the Greek does not help to determine whether this word relates to time or place. Possibly it may mean the PROVINCES OF EGYPT. See No. 5, 8, and 21, 44, where the two meanings both appear.

Line 22.

1   CHIEF; A,P,A, plural; ⲀⲠⲈ; as No. 8, 25. This helps to determine the meaning of the former word.

2   BECAUSE OF THIS; as No. 16, 45, &c.

3   EVENT; as No. 8, 12, and 20, 25. See No. 7, 32, for an explanation of the difficulty in regard to this word.

4   IF; as No. 20, 27; 19, 13, &c.

5   Is MADE; from the auxiliary verb, as No. 12, 38.

6   BEHOLD; as No. 21, 35, &c.

7   DECREE OR ARRANGEMENT; as No. 20, 36; but made into a verb by the help of the auxiliary verb, No. 22, 5, from which it is separated by the interjection. We must translate, " If the year shall be arranged."

8   The YEAR, that of the seasons; the Greek has ενιαυτος; but the Greek and hieroglyphics do not always agree in the use of the word.

9   THE; as No. 20, 14, &c.

10   DAY; as No. 20, 42, &c.

11   THREE HUNDRED; according to the Greek.

12   SIXTY. See No. 15, 24, for these numerals.

13   AND; as No. 18, 1, &c.

14   FIVE DAYS; as No. 20, 6.

15   NOTED, or *peculiar*, is the meaning that we must give to this word, which at No. 36, 6, is the *Pattern* marked on the holy cakes belonging to the priests.   These are the days called by the Greeks the Epagomenæ.   See the Calendar.

16   ORDERED; as No. 16, 47, and 35, 25.

17   ADDITIONAL; see No. 22, 36.

18   To BE ADDED; as No. 6, 30.   M is the prefix of the infinitive mood.   The first letter, the hind quarters of a lion, seems to be of the same force as the fore quarters.   Compare this word and No. 22, 37, each following the same word.   See No. 14, 36, for this verb.

19   The prefix of the infinitive mood to the next verb.   See No. 29, 24.

20   To CELEBRATE; as No. 17, 32.

21   The ADDITIONAL; as No. 22, 17, and 36.

22   DAY; as No. 22, 10.

23   ONE, or *first*; as No. 21, 21, &c.

24   OF; as No. 21, 19, &c.

25   The ASSEMBLY, or *festival*; as No. 21, 34, &c.

26   UNTO; as No. 18, 33, &c.

27   The GODS EUERGETÆ; as No. 18, 4, &c.

28   AWAY FROM; SII, A, N, literally, ꟽꟾꟾ *until*; but it is placed, as we should consider, too early in the sentence, and we must make use of it later.   See No. 14, 11, and 21, where this peculiarity is explained.

29   DAY; as No. 20, 42.

30   THAT, as No. 21, 1.

31   BECAUSE OF; as No. 21, 30.

32   The FOURTH YEAR; as No. 21, 31.

33   UNTIL; being the prefix of the case to the coming substantive, to mark it out as the word governed by the preposition *Until*,

No. 22, 28.   Or this letter may be described as the latter half of No. 22, 28, here repeated.

34   The ADDED; as No. 22, 17, but without the plural sign.

35   FIVE DAYS; as No. 22, 14.

36   ADDITIONAL; as No. 22, 34, &c.   This word may be taken as the well-known Greek name for those days, the *Epagomenæ*, which made the year of twelve months and five days.   These days were added to the Egyptian year at least as early as the year B.C. 1322.

37   Which were ADDED; as No. 22, 18, &c.

39   The NEW YEAR's DAY; as No. 3, 16, and 22, 15.

40   UPON; the preposition following its noun, as No. 12, 40.   See No. 7, 32.

41   So that IT MAY BE MADE; F,R,E; the auxiliary verb ɪpɪ, preceded by ϭ the sign of the third person singular.   This F, in Coptic, is a prefix; but in the hieroglyphics it is more usually a suffix, as at No. 7, 31.

42   KNOWN, according to the Greek; CII,N,B.   The word ⲬⲚⲞⲨ, *to know*, with B instead of F for the sign of the third person singular.

43   MEN and WOMEN; as No. 10, 34.

44   ALL; as No. 17, 7, &c.

45   ABOUT; as No. 15, 16, &c.

46   THIS; as No. 14, 18.   These two words may be compared also to No. 16, 45.

47   FORMER; N,E,T,O; from ⲈⲀⲦⲎ, *to precede*, with N the prefix of the past tense, as at No. 20, 23.

48   DEFECT; TII, R,?; perhaps ⲬⲞⲢⲈ *a defect*, the TII having the guttural force, as is not unusual.

49   Of the ARRANGEMENT; literally, APPOINTED WRITING; from ⲬⲰ *to appoint*, and the character for *Scribe* or *Writing*.   See No. 9, 10, for the force of the first letter, and No. 32, 16, for the word *Writing*.

50   IN RESPECT OF; N,T,R; ⲚⲦⲈⲢⲈ, *as, when*.

Line 23.

1   The CIVIL YEARS; as No. 1, 1, &c.; those of the reign used in dates.

2   AND; as No. 18, 1, &c.

3   The NATURAL YEAR; as No. 19, 23, &c.

4 ·   AND; as No. 18, 1, &c.

5   The COMMANDS; T; ⲦⲀⲨⲞ, *to tell*, explained by the D.S. of
a man pointing to his mouth. See No. 22, 16.

6   WHICH; as No. 22, 46, &c.

7   OF, or *relating to;* as No. 1, 8, &c.

8   Perhaps the JUDGMENTS; E,P,O, plural; perhaps ϨⲈⲡ, *a
judgment;* but this is not very satisfactory.

9   OF, or *relating to;* as No. 23, 7, &c.

10   The AMENDMENT; L, CH,O, plural; ⲖⲰⲬⲒ *to heal.* The
hieroglyphics make no distinction between an L and an R.

11   OF; N,E,M; ⲚⲈⲘ; as No. 2, 10.

12   The FAULTS; T,N,B, plural; perhaps from ⲚⲞⲂⲈ *a fault,*
with T, for the article prefixed in an unusual way. This is not
wholly satisfactory, as in Coptic our word is masculine, and T is
the feminine article. See No. 8, 2, for the letter B.

13   THE; as No. 20, 37.

14   HEAVENS; as No. 20, 38.

15   Which HAPPENED; as No. 21, 47.

16   To COME TO PASS; as No. 21, 48.

17   BEHOLD; as No. 21, 35, and 19, 8.

18   The PRODUCTION or COMMAND; as No. 22, 16, though with
different characters. See No. 5, 35, for the T, or rather TAU,
and No. 2, 10, for the vowel E, making together ⲦⲀⲨⲈ, *to beget.*

19   The ADORNMENTS. From ⲦⲎⲂ, *a finger,* we get ⲦⲀⲂⲦⲈⲂ
adorned.

20   SOLELY, or *singly,* as No. 9, 28.

21   The EXCELLENCE; H,O; ϨⲞⲨⲞ.

22   Of THE; as No. 20, 14, &c.

23   The GODS EUERGETÆ; as No. 22, 27, &c.

====

24   WHEREAS, or literally, *This,* as No. 22, 2, and No. 16, 45,
where we have *Whereas* written at full, as *Upon this.*

25   WHEN; S,K, it would seem, instead of ASK, No. 7, 30, &c.

26   A *daughter;* as No. 2, 5.

28   UNTO; H,R,N; ϨⲒⲢⲈⲚ, as No. 11, 38. See No. 7, 32.

29—36   KING PTOLEMY LIVING for EVER, BELOVED by PTHAH,
AND; as No. 11, 23—30.

37   QUEEN; NEB, TO; ΠΗß, ΘΟ; *Lord of the world,* since there
is no sign of the feminine.   To the dish we gave the force of NEB
at No. 5, 9; and to the latter characters the force of TO at
No. 1, 10.   This title NEB, seems to be allied to Nebo, the
name of the Babylonian god.

38   BERENICE; as No. 11, 32, &c.

39   The GODS EUERGETÆ; as No. 11, 33, &c.

40   The sitting figures of the king and queen, as the D.S.

41   UNTO THEM; II,T,T,O; ϪΑΤΟΤΟΥ *unto them.*   Compare
No. 12, 17, and No. 18, 18; where we have the preposition
without the final vowels, which are the personal pronoun.   As the
preposition is compounded of ΤΟΤ *a hand,* the artist chooses a
hand for his letter T, rather than any other form of that letter.

42   BERENICE; as No. 23, 38.   The young princess had the same
name as her mother.

43   THE; as No. 12, 30, &c.

44   NAME HER.   See No. 12, 25, for the word *Name.*   The final
S is the feminine pronoun suffix for *Her.*

45   IMMEDIATELY, as is required by the Greek.   See No. 14, 8,
and 14, 20, and 16, 21, in all of which places it bears a similar
meaning.

46   PROCLAIMED; O,S; ωω, *to proclaim.*

47   A queen.   See No. 4, 32.   But here we have not got the K
of the word Hyk; and we have the indefinite article prefixed.

Line 24.

1   D.S. of the queen, as at No. 4, 32.

2   BY, preposition, as No. 22, 45, &c.

3   FORTUNE or ACCIDENT; as No. 23, 16, and 13, 24, &c.

4   BEHOLD, as No. 19, 8, and 23, 17, &c.

5   The GODDESS.   See the word *God,* No. 5, 15.   It has here,
instead of the masculine termination, that for the feminine, as in
the queens' names.

6   The SAME; T,N; allied to ΤΑΝΑΙ, *in like manner,* and
ΤΕΝΤΩΝ, *to imitate,* see Voc. 1286.   Compare No. 20, 18.

7   LITTLE; A,O,S,M; ωΗω, *little,* preceded by the article,

which, according to custom, in Coptic, is joined to the adjective, or substantive, whichever stands first.

8   WOMAN; R,N,N; ⲣⲉⲙ, *a man*, or *woman*, followed by T,S the feminine termination of the queens' names, and by the D.S. In comparing the hieroglyphics with the Coptic, the change from N to M is not unusual. See No. 19, 43.

9   TAKEN AWAY; S, K,S; ⲥⲉⲕ, with a final S, which may be to make the adjective feminine. See No. 25, 31.

10   UNTO, preposition; as No. 15, 37, &c.

11   HEAVEN; P,T; ⲡⲏ, *heaven*, followed by the feminine article See No. 23, 14.

12   WHILST; M,S, CH, CH,T; a word which we may very satis factorily support by comparing it to ⲥⲁⳛⲏⲧ, *lower*, an ⲥⲁⳛⲟⲩⲛ *within*; having an M for the prefix.

13   The PRIESTS; as No. 1, 24, &c.

14   Who had COME; as No. 3, 9, where in the same way a characte with legs was chosen as figurative of motion, and to distinguis this word from others of the same letters.

15   From the COUNTRY; as No. 1, 10, &c.

16   NEAR; CH,R; ⲉⳛⲣⲏⲓ, *within*. See No. 35, 13.

17   The KING; as No. 1, 12, and 13, &c.

18   His PRESENCE; N,R,O, plural; ⲛⲓⲣⲱⲟⲩ, *the mouths*. Th *Mouth*, in Coptic is used for *He himself.*

19   YEARLY, literally, *year;* as No. 22, 8.

20   REMAINING, according to the Greek, M,E,B,T, with D.S. of house. M may be a prefix, and ⲉⲓⲉⲃⲧ is *to rise;* but this wi hardly help to support our rendering.

21   In the PRESENCE, as No. 24, 18, but rathered shortened in th number of letters, as is not unusual when a word is used a secon time in the sentence. See No. 6, 30, where these same letter are the prefix of the imperfect tense.

22   Of HIS MAJESTY; as No. 3, 18, &c.

23   CELEBRATING, is the meaning here required, though No. 12, 5, we considered this word a pronoun. The first lette EI, may represent ⲁⲓⲁⲓ, *to magnify*, or it may be made to star for the word IOT, of No. 18, 31, &c. See No. 29, 13, whe we must give the same meaning to the single letter.

24   THE ; using the heavens for a P, from ⲚⲎ, *the heavens*. This is as remarkable a use of a character as what we saw at No. 21, 30, where the figure of Osiris was used for *Because of.*

25   GREAT ; according to the Greek ; R, CH,T ; which drives us to the rather unreasonable conjecture that the sculptor has reversed the order of the letters, and that they are meant for ⲬⲰⲢⲓ, *great*, with T the feminine article, as No. 4, 2. We made the same bold conjecture at No. 8, 26 ; and at No. 2, 7, it was certainly the case in the name of Philammon.

26   LAMENTATION, literally, *Cutting ;* SH, T ; ⲩⲉⲧ, *to cut.* The custom of gashing the flesh in grief was common in Egypt, and deprives this rendering of any improbability. It is described by Herodotus in *lib.* II., 61. For the force of our first letter see No. 1, 31 ; 5, 16 ; and 16, 34.

27   THE ; as No. 20, 14, &c.

28   PRAISES ; A,E ; from ⲀⲓⲀⲓ, *to praise*, as No. 7, 1. Compare No. 24, 23.

29   HE, but meaning *They ;* as No. 4, 37.

30   Perhaps FINDING ; H ; ⲅⲉ *to find.* The Greek has " Thinking it right." Perhaps we must understand our word as *Considering.* This character is common as ⲅⲉ, *like ;* see No. 16, 40, &c.

31   ABOUT, or *Upon ;* as No. 13, 22, &c. See No. 7, 32, for an explanation of this word.

32   PARTICULARS ; at No. 9, 28, and 23, 20, this is rendered *Single things.*

33   HE, meaning *They ;* as No. 24, 29, &c.

34   ASKED ; ?,H,O, with D.S. of a man holding up his hands in the act of prayer ; probably, ⲧⳟⲟ, *to ask.* The lessusual Coptic letter is naturally represented by an unusual character.

35   FROM ; as No. 4, 3. See also No. 2, 10, for this compound character.

36   The KING, here described by only one of his two titles. See No. 1, 12, and 13. The figure placed as D.S. holds in his hand the whip carried by Osiris, as if it were in his character as a god that he undertook to declare his infant daughter a goddess.

37   AND ; as No. 23, 36, &c.

38   QUEEN; as No. 4, 82, and with the same D.S.

39   THE; as No. 28, 43, &c.

40   GIFTS; as No. 5, 35. But here either the termination is incomplete, or it is in a less usual form. See, however, Voc. 401 for the same. It is probable that, as the whole sentence is written by the help of the ear, without any attempt to spell grammatically, the N of the plural termination is dropt, because the following word begins with an M. For other cases of the same kind, see No. 7, 5; 18, 12; and 32, 4, in all of which it is doubtful whether the M holds the place of a final N, or of a preposition following the word in which the N has been dropt.

41   FROM; as No. 21, 27, &c.

42   THEM; as No. 9, 4.

43   To GRANT; the word *Give* preceded by R,R, which may be ЄⲂⲢⲎⲒ the preposition, as we interpret the double R, at No. 10, 26; and 20, 24; and may thus form part of the verb.

Line 25.

1   To CONSECRATE; O,T,P; ⲞⲨⲞⲦЄⲂ. See Voc. 438. This word forms the end of many Egyptian names, such as Amunothph, *dedicated to Amun ;* and Mandothph, *dedicated to Mandoo.*

2   A GODDESS; as No. 24, 5.

3   The SAME; T,N; ⲦЄⲚⲦⲰⲚ, *to imitate ;* as No. 24, 6.

4   LIKE; Ⲥ̨Є *like ;* though more often used in this inscription as ⲀⲤ̨Ⲁ *and.*

5   OSIRIS. The Egyptian sculptors take some liberties, for pictorial reasons, when writing this word. The hatchet is *God.* The throne is ISI, as in the name of the goddess Isis. The eye is used for R, instead of the mouth, and in this word only. In every other word the eye is a vowel, as in the name *Arsinoe,* and at No. 12, 5; and 14, 1, and 15, 20, and 16, 22, and 17, 33, &c. But in order, probably, to represent the eye of providence, the sculptor here uses it instead of the mouth. It forms the word of action ⲒⲢⲒ, while the ISI is Ⲱ̨Ⲩ, *to declare.* Hence the name Osiris, a *Judgment-maker,* or Judge, a that of the Cabeiri gods means *Punishment-makers,* from Ⲕ̨ⲂⲀ, *to punish.*

6   IN; as No. 18, 40 &c.

7   TEMPLE; as No. 4, 9.

8   OF; as No. 1, 8, &c.

9   CANOPUS, according to the Greek; P,K,O,T, followed by the feminine article, and D.S. of a city. But this reading of the letters is given in the belief that the second letter should have been like the K in No. 6, 3; whereas it too much resembles the N in No. 6, 30. See No. 4, 14.

10   WHICH; as No. 22, 3.

11   AMONG; a compound preposition, formed of M, ⲙ, in, and N,E,N; ⲛⲅⲟⲩⲛ, within. See No. 25, 34.

12   The TEMPLES; as No. 5, 4, &c.

13   PRINCIPAL, according to the Greek; literally, ROYAL; as No. 26, 15, and No. 37, 24, where its meaning is very certainly proved. But see also No. 8, 21 and No. 13, 48, where it of necessity bears a very different meaning. Having the original force of ⲉⲡⲱⲧⲉ, milk, it here means ⲟⲩⲡⲟ, royal, and there ⲉⲣⲟⲩⲟⲧ, happiness.

14   FOR WHICH, two words, as No. 16, 45, &c.

15   EXPENSE; S,O; ⲟⲟ, as No. 25, 18.

16   GREAT; as No. 4, 2; 5, 2; &c.

17   Of the EGYPTIANS. See No. 8, 31, &c. where this word is spelt with fewer letters. This is perhaps the adjective, not Copts, but Coptic, in the plural.

18   EXPENSE; as No. 25, 15.

19   FOR THEM; M,T,T; of which M is the preposition, and TT is ⲧⲟⲧ the hand. In Coptic it is written with an N, ⲛⲧⲟⲧⲟⲩ, literally, For their hand; but the pronoun at the end of the word is omitted, as we must suppose, in carelessness.

20   Was PREPARED, as No. 5, 11, and 30, 38.

21   BY; as No. 25, 8, with a different meaning. But the Coptic use of the prepositions is very irregular.

22   The KING; as No. 24, 36.

23   AND; as No. 4, 31, &c., where it is rendered Likewise.

24   The LIVING MEN and WOMEN; as No. 7, 20, &c.

25   OF; as No. 11, 17, &c.

26   The COUNTRY; as 24, 15, &c.

27   IN or *during ;* as No. 21, 7, &c.

28   The TIMES; as No. 11, 7, &c.

29   The auxiliary verb; A,R; ιpι; as No. 22, 5. It is part of
the coming verb.

30   BEHOLD, as No. 22, 6, &c.

31   SHALL DRAW; S,K; cεK, as at No. 24, 9. It is separated
from its auxiliary verb, No. 25, 29, by the word *Behold.* Without
the auxiliary verb it might be a substantive.

32   Perhaps OUR; T,O,N; ⊖ωn, *our.* It is the adjective to the
foregoing word, which thus becomes, " *We* shall draw."

33   OSIRIS; as No. 25, 5.

34   DURING or AMONG ; as No. 25, 11.

35   The DRAWING ALONG; S,K ; cεK, as No. 25, 31. The final
TT may be τοτ, *a hand,* a word so often used as a preposition,
and here it may correspond to our *Along.*

36   The BARGE, represented pictorially. The procession of men
drawing along the statues of the gods in a barge on the Nile,
may be seen on the sarcophagus, Egypt. Inscrip. pl. 28.

37   To, a preposition ; as No. 25, 27, &c.

38   The TEMPLE; as No. 25, 7.

39   SAME ; as No. 24, 6 ; being an adjective to the word which it
follows.

40   AT or ON ; as No. 25, 27, &c.

41   The SEASON, as No. 21, 20, &c.

42   OF; as No. 23, 7, &c.

43   The YEAR; as No. 1, 1, &c.

44   FROM; as No. 20, 9.

45   The TEMPLE; as No. 25, 38 ; but without the D.S. which
follows it, and seems very unnecessary to a character which is
itself pictorial.

46   WHICH; as No. 23, 6, though with different characters. The
T being below the N is considered as following it.

47   HERACLEIUM, according to the Greek. The town of Hera-
cleopolis, near which this temple was situated, was in the middle
of Egypt, and was near the town, or perhaps was the same town
as that which was fortified by the Ptolemies, and called Ptolemais.

It was within a few miles of Oxyrynchus, where the fish was worshipped; and this helps to explain the hieroglyphical name where we see a fish among the characters. The first three letters are A,N,R, or more probably A, CH,R, as these two characters are easily mistaken; ⲬⲰⲢⲒ, *great*, the Egyptian name for Hercules. The next letter, B, may represent such a word as ABO, *city*; as we judge from the names of many Egyptian cities. Thus Bubastis is *the city of Pasht*; Bu-siris is *the city of Osiris*. The two other letters, M,R, may be the name of the sacred fish. Or the M may be the prefix of the case, and R alone the word *Fish*.

Line 26.

1   ON or *in*; as No. 25, 6.

2   The month of CHOIAC, the fourth in the Egyptian civil year; and therefore, when the Calendar was arranged, B.C. 1322, and when it again became right in A.D. 138, it began on our 16th of October. At this time, however, when Payni, the tenth month, began on the 19th of July, Choiac of the civil year began on the 20th of January. See the Calendar.

3   TWENTY-NINE; the numerals, as No. 15, 42. This day, the day of the ceremony of the water procession on the Nile, was probably the time of the priests' assembling at Canopus; and the Decree probably means by this month, not the Choiac of the civil year, but of the reformed calendar which the priests are now proposing to introduce. The 29th of Choiac was eighteen days before the 17th of Tybi, when the Decree was issued.

4   THE EGYPTIANS; as No. 8, 31, but preceded by the article. Instead of this, the Greek has *The priests of the course.*

5   Of the TEMPLES; as No. 25, 12, &c.

6   PRINCIPAL; as No. 25, 13, and No. 26, 15, where the Greek supports this meaning.

7   AT; as No. 25, 27, &c.

8   The TIMES; as No. 25, 28, &c. It ends with plural letters, S,N.

9   THE; as No. 23, 43, &c.; or perhaps THEY, as No. 24, 29, if the following word is a verb.

10   COMPLETE THE SACRIFICES; E,I,K, for ⲆⲒⲔ, *a dedication*; and

R,R, the auxiliary verb of action, ΙΡΙ; and followed by a burning censer, the D.S. See No. 32, 43.

11   THE; as No. 24, 39, &c.

12   ALTARS; SII, E,O; ϢΗΟΥΙ, followed by the D.S. See No. 20, 15.

13   OF; as No. 25, 25, &c.

14   The TEMPLES; as No. 25, 12, &c.

15   PRINCIPAL, so rendered in the Greek. See No. 25, 13, and 37, 24.

16   THE; as No. 26, 11, &c.

17   ONE HALF OF THE COURSE, according to the Greek. This is probably some standard carried in the procession of the priests at the top is an ostrich feather.

18   THE OTHER HALF OF THE COURSE; perhaps a similar standard.

19   OF; as No. 26, 1, &c.

20   Perhaps FAMILY; in the Greek, *course*. But whether is thereby meant the procession or the tribe of priests is doubtful. The letters are CH, F,T. The T may be the feminine article. The word ΧΗϦ, like the Hebrew גאל, means at once the *Avenger* *Redeemer*, and *Next of Kin*; and as the priesthood in Egypt was hereditary, it may well be rendered *Family*. See No. 34, 51 Compare also No. 8, 17.

21   THE meaning *Those*; as No. 26, 9, &c.

22   OF; as No 22, 33, &c.

23   TEMPLE; as No. 25, 7, &c.

24   THAT SAME; as No. 24, 6, &c.

25   MINGLING or JOINING; M,O, CH,T; ΜΟΥΧΤ, *mixed*. The Greek, μιτα δι ταυτα, which should mean *After this*, may have been understood by the Egyptian scribe to mean *Jointly with this*.

26   In this not uncommon word Dr. Reinisch's copy has the twig with four leaves on each; but I correct it with confidence, and adopt Dr. Lepsius's reading. The twig with four leaves is S, from ϬΕ *a plant*, as at No. 1, 12, &c. The twig with two leaves is C perhaps from ΟΚΕ, ΔΚΕ, ΔΧΙ, *a reed*, as at No. 11, 1, and No. 33, 15. This word O,O,N,N, I read in other inscriptions OΥϢΙΝΙ *shining*; see Voc. 658; but here it may mean HARP as that Coptic word has this second meaning also.

27   ALL the OTHER; see No. 16, 27, &c., *Other;* and No. 16, 28, &c., *All.*

28   RELIGIOUS CEREMONIES; as No. 20, 22, and 22, 20, &c.

29   FOR; as No. 25, 42.

30   The CELEBRATIONS; as No. 19, 33, but with the omission of a vowel, and the addition of the plural sign. It is not unusual, when a word is often repeated, to find fewer letters in the later examples.

31   DEDICATION; as No. 26, 10, but written with fewer letters, as explained above.

32   HER RAISING UP; EI, N,S; from ꙇℕꙇ *to raise,* with S, the feminine pronoun.

33   The GODDESS; or literally, *God,* as we have no feminine termination. The D.S. is of a woman, as No. 24, 8, &c.

34   Probably MADE FOR HER; T,R,S; the TR means Ⲧⲣⲟ, *to make,* and the S, the feminine termination, may be *for her.* This is not wholly satisfactory, but it seems confirmed at No. 28, 48, and 29, 15. But see No. 36, 24, where TR is translated *All.*

35   Probably LIBATION, or PURIFICATION; the character which we have so often rendered *Priest.* This character, when it means a Libation, should be followed by the D.S. of water. See Voc. 347, 353, and 361.

36   To HEAL; S,N; ⳫⲒℕꙇ; as No. 29, 17.

37   The GRIEF FOR HER; in Coptic ⲓⲓⲕⲁⳫ. This may be explained if we suppose the locks of hair to be ⲕⲁⳫⲓ, *the head.* The final S may be the feminine pronoun, to make it *Grief for her,* as No. 29, 18. But see No. 22, 48, where the lock of hair seems to be an II.

38   HER RAISING UP; as No. 26, 32.

Line 27.

1   They PREPARED; as No. 5, 11; though here we have an R more than in the former place. It may perhaps be the preposition, possibly *For.*

2   THEY, or THEM; as No. 9, 4.

3   WITH; as No. 26, 19, &c.

4   PERSEVERANCE; S,R,F; ⲥⲉⲣⳅⲉ, *to persevere.*

5   Possibly CARE, as such a meaning is here required. It may be a flame of fire, as at No. 26, 10; and the word ⲱⲁⲃ, is both *Flame* and *Care*.

6   LIKE; as No. 16, 40. But see No. 24, 30, where we find this letter with a different meaning.

7   The CEREMONIES, or PREPARATION, or some such meaning, is here needed; but the Greek does not help us.

8   THE; as No. 23, 43, &c. Here the scribe follows the Greek so closely that he puts the article before Apis, and not before Mnevis.

9   APIS THE BULL; as No. 5, 26.

10   MNEVIS THE BULL; as No. 5, 27.

11   CELEBRATED; as No. 24, 23.

=

12   It was DETERMINED, S,M,M,M; ⲥⲓⲛⲉ, *to declare*.

13   THERE WAS GIVEN; N,R,T,T; the word to *Give*, as No. 5, 35, preceded by NRT, a prefix for the imperfect tense, which we may support by the Coptic, ⲛⲉⲡⲉⲧⲉⲛ, of the second person plural.

14   BY or UPON; as No. 13, 22, and 24, 31, &c.

15   COMMAND; T, with D.S. of a man speaking; perhaps ⲧⲁⲩⲟ, as No. 23, 5.

16   HONOURS. See No. 5, 13, where we supposed that Colossal Statues were the honours meant. The final TN is in place of the more usual SN.

17   IMMORTAL; as No. 1, 16, &c. The adjective follows its substantive.

18   UNTO; as No. 26, 22, &c.

19   The QUEEN; as No. 4, 32; but having also the final S, the feminine termination. This title, given to one who died in infancy, would be more suitably rendered *Princess;* but with the Greeks of Alexandria the words Βασιλευς and Βασιλισσα were given to the members of the royal family, without any reference to sovereignty over a state.

20   BERENICE; as No. 23, 42.

21   The DAUGHTER; as No. 23, 26.

22   OF; as No. 27, 18, &c.

23   The GODS EUERGETÆ; as No. 23, 23, &c.

24   In ; as No. 5, 3, &c.

25   The temples ; as No. 5, 4, &c.

26   Of ; as No. 5, 5, &c.

27   The country ; as No. 5, 6, &c.

28   At the times ; as No. 26, 8 ; but with the article, and without the preposition before it.

29   At ; as No. 26, 7, and 25, 27, &c.

30   Which ; as No. 23, 6, &c.

31   Once upon a time ; as No. 8, 20, and 21, 49, &c.

32   Probably, She was taken up. In No. 24, 9, we have what seems to be this word written S,K,S ; here we have the K omitted. The figure of the bird, and the sense required, lead us to conjecture that this is an omission caused by accident, or haste. See also No. 28, 3, for the same word without the feminine pronoun postfixed.

33   Among ; E,M,M, or M,E,M ; probably ꟿꟾꟾ, *with;* the M being used for N, as is not unusual.

34   The gods ; as No. 5, 15 ; but here we have the plural formed, not by repeating the word, but by three dots.

35   In ; as No. 27, 24, &c.

36   The month of Tybi ; as No. 1, 6.

37   The month in which ; as No. 3, 24.

Line 28.

1   Ra, the *Sun*, the great god of Thebes ; R,E ; ꟼꟾ.

2   Himself ; P,O ; literally, *The one;* ꟼ the article and Oꟻꟽꟸ, *one.*

3   Took up ; as No. 24, 9.

4   The daughter of Ra. See No. 27, 21, *Daughter ;* in addition to which, we have the figure of the sun, ornamented with a sacred asp. In Wilkinson's *Materia Hierog.* I. ix. we have an inscription in honour of this goddess: " Hecate, the illustrious daughter of Ra." The name *Hecate,* is the feminine of ꟼꟾꟶ, *a sorcerer,* and is spelt with the D.S. of our No. 35, 7, preceded with T, the feminine article. The word *Illustrious* is our No. 26, 26.

5   To ; as No. 24, 10 ; 27, 29, &c.

6   The heavens ; as No. 24, 11 ; but here we have the article prefixed to the noun, as No. 20, 37, and 38.

H

7 Is CELEBRATED; as No. 3, 19, and No. 28, 43. The final F
is the suffix of the third person singular.

8 WHO; as No. 16, 8, and No. 28, 6, where it is used as the
article.

9 UNTO HIM; H,T,F; ૬ⲁⲧⲉ૬.

10 SHE WAS; N,S; ⲛⲉⲥ, being in Coptic used as a prefix to the
word *Named*, which is to follow.

11 The APPLE OF THE EYE, expressed pictorially.

12 AND; H; ⲁ૬ⲁ.

13 THE; N,T; ⲛⲉⲧ, *who*, but only in the plural. It is here used
for ⲡⲉⲧ.

14 SACRED ASP, being the figure of the asp, which was tied by a
ribband as an ornament to the forehead of the kings and statues
of the gods. In the Greek it is called the Diadem, or Crown.

15 OF; as No. 27, 24, &c.

16 HIS HEAD; the animal's head is followed by T, the feminine
article to the word ⲁⲡⲉ *head;* and then by F, the pronoun *His*.

17 THE; as No. 23, 43, &c.

18 HER NAME; as No. 23, 44. Thus the words *The her name*,
seem treated as a verb, and with the prefix No. 28, 10, become
She was named.

19 THE; as No. 28, 17, &c.

20 BELOVED; M,R; ⲙⲉⲣⲉ, *to love.* See No. 2, 13, for this
form of M.

21 This sitting figure of a man, with his hand to his mouth, must
here be held to be symbolical of kissing, following, as it does, the
word *Beloved.* At No. 27, 15, &c., it was the D.S. of speaking.

22 BY; as No. 26, 29, &c.

23 HER FATHER. Compare No. 4, 4, *Father*, which is there
written with three letters instead of our single F, and followed
by *His*, instead of *Her*. The writer would seem in many places
to use fewer letters in each word, towards the latter part of the
inscription, than he did towards the beginning.

24 They shall CELEBRATE; as No. 21, 36; 21, 41, &c.

25 UNTO, preposition; as No. 28, 22, &c.

26 HER; being a suffix to the preposition, as at No. 28, 23.

27   ASSEMBLIES; as No. 21, 34, &c.

28   BY, or WITH, preposition; as No. 28, 22, &c.

29   WATER PROCESSION, represented pictorially by a pair of arms holding an oar. In the Rosetta Stone a similar character means *Sculptured* or a *Statue*, as the arms are then supposed to hold a chisel.

30   IN, FROM, or UNTO; preposition, as No. 28, 15, &c.

31   The SANCTUARY; or inner room of a temple; as No. 16, 32.

32   GREAT, in the plural; as No. 5, 2, &c.

33   The GREATER PART, according to the Greek; CH, T; KⲰⲦⲈ *fulness*, or perhaps simply KⲈⲦ, *the others*, as it is translated at No. 30, 7.

34   Of the TEMPLES. This is the word No. 25, 12, written with another form of the M, and repeated three times, instead of being followed by three dots. These three words, *Great, fulness, temples*, are the rude translation of πλειοσιν ιεροις. Such a comparison of the two shows that the Greek was the original, and the Hieroglyphics the translation.   •

35   OF THE FIRST RANK; as No. 25, 13, &c.

36   IN; preposition, as No. 28, 15, &c.

37   MONTH; a moon, followed R,E, for the D.S. of time, as No. 17, 6, but with the omission of two of the letters. As the words become repeated, they are written in shorter form.

38   THAT; as No. 22, 30, &c.

39   When the MAKING; some part of ⲓⲡⲓ, *to make*, as at No. 17, 33, and 18, 25, &c.

40   A GODDESS; as No. 26, 33, and without the feminine termination to the word.

41   OF; as No. 28, 22, &c.

42   The QUEEN. The word is composed of the sceptre which forms part of No. 1, 11, *Reign;* and of No. 3, 18, *His Majesty;* and this is followed by S, the feminine termination, or pronoun, and the D.S. of a woman.

43   Is CELEBRATED; as No. 28, 7, and No. 29, 19.

44   In ADDITION; as No. 15, 3; and as No. 14, 35, and 36, in a fuller form.

45   There SHALL BE CELEBRATED; as No. 17, 32, and 33, where, however, it is written with several more letters.

46   An ASSEMBLY; as No. 28, 27, &c.

47   ONE; as No. 19, 39, &c.

48   There SHALL BE MADE; T,R; ⲦⲢⲞ, *to make*; as No. 26, 34. But see No. 18, 8, where these letters are the word ⲦⲎⲢ, *all*.

49   A WATER PROCESSION; as No. 28, 29.

50   ONE; as No. 28, 47.

51   UNTO; as No. 28, 25, &c.

52   QUEEN; as No. 27, 19, &c.

53   BERENICE; as No. 27, 20, &c.

54   DAUGHTER; as No. 27, 21.

Line 29.

1   OF; as No. 27, 22.

2   The GODS EUERGETÆ; as No. 27, 23, &c.

3   IN; as No. 27, 24, &c.

4   The TEMPLES; as No. 27, 25, &c.

5   OF; as No. 27, 26, &c.

6   The TWO REGIONS, meaning Upper and Lower Egypt, as at No. 10, 44; and No. 18, 7; but here, after the name has been written several times, the D.S. is thought sufficient.

7   IN; as No. 26, 7, &c.

8   The TIMES; as No. 26, 8, &c.

9   OF; as No. 29, 3, &c.

10   The month of TYBI; as No. 27, 36.

11   FROM; SH, A,N; ⲱⲁⲛ, *when.*

12   The SEVENTEETH DAY; the numerals, as No. 15, 42, preceded by the D.S. for *Time*, instead of the word *Day*.

13   Probably WAS KEPT or *celebrated*. The Eye here seems used for the whole word, No. 28, 24, which has been so often written that now it is thought enough to carve the first letter only. See the abridgment at No. 28, 45, where the same first letter is used for a different word. See No. 24, 23, for the same difficulty.

14   HER WATER PROCESSION; as No. 28, 49. The final S may be *Her.*

15   WAS MADE for HER; as No. 26, 34; and as No. 28, 48, without the pronoun.

16   A LIBATION OF PURIFICATION; as No. 26, 35.

17   To HEAL; as No. 26, 36.

18   GRIEF FOR HER; as No. 26, 37.

19   WAS CELEBRATED; as No. 19, 42, &c.

20   As ON THE DAY, is the meaning here required. The last character is the D.S. for DAY. The letters M,S,E, may be a preposition.

21   FIRST; literally, the *Head*; A,P; ⲀⲠⲈ, *a head.*

22   DURING; OUB, I,RO. A compound preposition, ⲞⲨⲂⲈ, *through*, and R, as No. 26, 7. The first character usually represents ⲞⲨⲀⲂ, *good, holy.* See No. 14, 1.

23   FOUR DAYS; see No. 22, 35.

=

24   To SET UP; M, the prefix of the infinitive mood, as at No. 17, 32; T,O,T, ⲦⲞⲨⲰⲦ, *an image*; followed by S, which may be the feminine sign, as it is the statue of the princess; and ending with the D.S. of something erected. At No. 22, 19, and 20, this word, without the D.S., is rendered *to celebrate.*

25   A SACRED STATUE; being the word *God*, the systrum, or musical instrument, which the statue is to hold, and the D.S. of a woman, as it is to be the statue of a woman.

26   UNTO; as No. 29, 1, &c.

27   The GODDESS; as No. 26, 33, but with the addition of the usual feminine termination, which is there wanting.

28   The SAME; as No. 26, 24; the adjective following its substantive.

29   OF; as No. 29, 3, &c.

30   GOLD; being an ornamental dish or basket in which gold rings are carried by men bringing tribute to the King in the sculptures of Thothmosis III. Moreover, at No. 5, 9, we showed that a dish was NEB, and hence represented ⲚⲞⲨⲂ, *gold.*

31   POLISHED; H,M; ⲈⲰⲒⲒ, *to polish.* This may describe the precious stones. On the other hand, it might be taken as two words, H, *and*, and M, *of.*

32　STONES; SH, T; ϣⲟⲧ, *hard*, followed by the D.S. of a stone. See No. 1, 31, for the force of the first letter.

33　ALL; as No. 5, 23.

34　A figure of the statue, which has been described. We might suppose the final S was added because it was the statue of a woman; but we have the same final S following the same figure where the statue is that of a king. There, however, it is described as a portable statue, as this, which was to be made of gold, of course was. Hence that final S belongs to some word which so describes the kind of image. See Rosetta Stone, line 8.

35　IN; as No. 29, 3.

36　The TEMPLES; as No. 27, 25. Compare No. 28, 34. There each character is repeated three times; here one only is so repeated, the other has the three dots.

37　Of FIRST RANK; compare No. 29, 40.

38　IN; as No. 29, 35, &c.

39　The TEMPLES; as No. 29, 36, or rather as No. 28, 34.

40　Of SECOND RANK.

41　AT; as No. 29, 7, &c.

42　The TIMES; as No. 29, 8, &c.

43　This word, R,T,E, seems to be the auxiliary verb ⲑⲣⲉ with the letters in a different order, and thus it forms part of the following word, as No. 37, 16. But see No. 11, 13, where we render it *a Reason*.

Line 30.

1　To CONSECRATE; M,T,E, FO; ⲙⲉⲧⲧⲟⲩⲃⲟ, *purity*, and with the foregoing auxiliary verb, *to purify*.

2　IN; as No. 29, 38, &c.

3　The HOLY PLACE; ⲉⲛ τῳ ἁγίῳ, that is probably in the temple proper, or house, as opposed to the temple-yard, which is what is usually meant in this Decree by the word *Temple*. The Greek distinguishes between the ἰερον, or *temple-yard*, including the House; the ἁγιον, the *holy* building or house; and the ἀδυτον, the *inner chamber*, the sanctuary, or holy of holies.

4　The PRIEST; as No. 2, 19; followed by the D.S.

5   The PROPHET, being the adjective to the foregoing substantive; R,O,E; from ⲣⲱ, *a mouth.*

6   The sacred BARGE, but possibly meaning another person, the *priest of the barge,* as a number of priests are here mentioned.

7   The OTHER; CH, T; ⲕⲉⲧ, *other.* See No. 28, 33; also No. 3, 5, for another form of the word.

8   PRIESTS; as No. 1, 24, &c.

9   CHOSEN; as No. 15, 26; though there we have an M as a prefix.

10   Of the PURIFICATIONS, as represented by the fire and water. See No. 16, 23; and also No. 2, 21, where it seems to mean *priests of the libations,* and is without the D.S. of water.

11   GREAT; as No. 25, 16, &c.; the adjective to the foregoing substantive.

12   The indefinite article to the following substantive; as No. 5, 7, &c.; or, possibly, AND; as No. 2, 3, &c.

13   Those who SING PRAISES; as No. 2, 22.

14   Of the GODS; as No. 27, 34.

15   THOSE WHO ROBE THE GODS; as No. 3, 2.

16   HE SHALL TAKE or CARRY; S, MES,A,F; from ⲙⲁϣ, *to take,* with S the prefix of the future tense, as at No. 20, 39, and 21, 4, &c.; and with F the suffix of the third person singular. That the first character is MES, see the name of Meshophra Thothmosis I., called Mesaphris by Manetho; also the well-known title over a king's second name of Lord of Battles, from ⲙⲁϣ, *to strike,* translated by Hermapion as Brave in War. It is the picture of ⲙⲏϣ, *an anvil.*

17   IT; the article, which we have only seen used in the nominative case; but at No. 34, 10, it is used for *Her,* in the objective case.

18   In HIS TWO ARMS; H,P,T; ϩⲡⲱⲧ a measure of length from finger to finger when the arms are stretched out.

19   The D.S. to the foregoing word. In other places in this inscription this character means *Fortune* or *Accident,* No. 8, 16, and 13, 24, &c. This perhaps may be explained by supposing that the resemblance between ϩⲡⲱⲧ, *the two arms,* and ϩⲱⲧⲡ, *to fall down,* or *happen,* was near enough to allow one to represent the other.

20   So that it MAY BE SEEN; see No. 37, 18, where it is rendered *Conspicuous* in the Greek.

21   ON or *in;* as No. 30, 2, where the M is of another form.

22   The DAY; as at No. 29, 23, &c.

23   OF; as No. 28, 41, &c.

24   The TAKING UP or *carrying out;* as No. 30, 16, but with the grammatical prefix and suffix. In the Greek we have the *Going out,* meaning the going out of the statues of the gods, which is here called the *Carrying out.*

25   AND; as No. 25, 4, &c.

26   ASSEMBLIES; as No. 28, 46, &c.

27   OF; as No. 29, 5, &c.

28   The GOD, the singular of No. 30, 14. The god meant may be Osiris, by the side of whose statue that of the princess was to be placed; but the Greek has *The other gods;* and in the Hieroglyphics the singular is often used for the plural.

29   IN; as No. 29, 7, &c.

30   The TIMES; as No. 29, 8, &c.

31   BY; as No. 18, 44; 22, 45, &c.

32   THIS; as No. 18, 45; 22, 46, &c.

33   SEEN, according to the Greek; but the force of the character is uncertain.

34   By ALL; N,E,B; ⲚⲒⲂⲓ, as No. 37, 32.

35   MEN and WOMEN; as No. 7, 26, &c.

36   ALL ; as No. 20, 21, &c., but with the addition of S,N, for the plural. This is the adjective to the foregoing substantive, notwithstanding the word by which it is preceded.

37   WORSHIP; represented by a man throwing himself on the ground.

38   IS TO BE PAID; as No. 5, 11 and 25, 20. Here our word begins with M, the prefix of the infinitive mood, and ends with F, the pronoun.

39   Perhaps AT ONCE, literally, *endeavouring* or *putting out the hand;* H,T,O,T ; ⲈⲒⲦⲞⲦ ; as No. 13, 15, and 18, 18, and 12, 17. This word seems often to be almost an unnecessary expletive, that only adds emphasis. See No. 36, 9, where it is also redundant.

40   UNTO; as No. 27, 22, &c.
41   The DISTINGUISHED or CONSPICUOUS; as No. 20, 26, &c.
42   BERENICE; as No. 28, 53, &c.

Line 31.

1   How, or *in like manner*; H,N,A, Ϩιnδ or Ϩιnδι.
2   The QUEEN; being the D.S. of a woman, as throughout in this inscription, and not distinguished by any mark of royalty from the next D.S.
3   Of WOMEN; as No. 24, 8.
4   Is CARRIED OUT; as No. 30, 24.
=
5   BEHOLD; as No. 23, 17, &c.   But these two letters may possibly belong one to the former and one to the following word.
6   It is DECREED, as No. 21, 8, &c.
7   THE, as No. 28, 17, &c.
8   CROWN; being a human head, but too small to show the ornaments upon it.
9   UPON; as No. 30, 40.
10   The SACRED STATUE; as No. 29, 25.
11   THAT; as No. 28, 38, &c.
12   NOT FROM; or, according to the Greek, *Not less than*.   See No. 19, 25, *Nothing*.   The M may be the preposition.
13   The RELIGIOUS CEREMONIES; as No. 4, 7, and 19, 1.
14   DECREED or APPOINTED; as No. 31, 6; and preceded by R, the auxiliary verb of action, as No. 21, 32.
15   THE CROWN; being the two words No. 31, 7, and 8; and in each case without the final vowel.   The artist shortens his words when they occur a second time.
16   Of the STATUES, meaning probably the little portable statues, each within a small shrine or temple, about 18 inches high; R,P, followed by T,S, the feminine termination of a woman's name, and then by D.S. of the statue; ϵρπϵ, the *sanctuary* of a temple.
17   OF; as No. 28, 41, &c.
18   HER MOTHER.   The vulture, the syllable MAU, is often used with this meaning, either with or without a final T for the article. Our final S is the pronoun *Her*.

19   The QUEEN, being the hawk with the feminine article, and thus the feminine of the word Pharaoh. See the use of the hawk in No. 3, 18, *His majesty*. Thus, though in the Greek, mother and infant daughter have the same title, they are very different in the Hieroglyphics.

20   BERENICE ; as No. 27, 20, &c.

21   It is to be PLACED. This is the word which we have repeatedly rendered *Kept, Held*, or *Celebrated*, as of a festival. See No. 19, 33, where, as here, it is preceded by the auxiliary verb of action.

22   CONSPICUOUSLY ; as No. 20, 26, &c.

23   WITH ; the preposition M, as No. 29, 38, &c. ; but of the form used in No. 29, 39.

24   EARS OF CORN ; SH, M,S, followed by the D.S. ; ϩⲉⲙⲥ, *an ear of corn*.

25   Two ; S,N, with two dots, as the D.S. ; ⲥⲛⲁⲩ, *two*. The form of the S is unusual ; compare it with that in No. 1, 29.

26   AN ASP ; the figure of the animal, preceded by the indefinite article.

27   On THE BACK ; CH, T, with S,N, for the plural ; ⲕⲟⲧ, *to turn round*.

28   A SCEPTRE ; the figure preceded by the indefinite article.

29   OF ; as No. 30, 40, &c.

30   PAPYRUS FLOWERS. The first letter, SH, represents these plants ; it is followed by I, and then by the D.S.

31   Perhaps To BE HELD UP ; M, the prefix of the infinitive mood ; K, ⲕⲁ, *to place*, and the D.S. of a man holding up. The value of the final S does not appear. The Greek has *To be of the same height* ; and that thought seems to be intended by the man's action.

32   The PAPYRUS PLANT ; as No. 31, 30, but written with fewer letters.

33   The CROWN ; as No. 31, 8.

34   The ASP ; as No. 31, 26.

35   THE SAME ; as 29, 28, &c.

36   LIKE ; as No. 27, 6, and 16, 40.

37   What is ACCUSTOMED or *customary* ; literally, *Heard* ; SOT, M ; CⲰTEⲖⲖ, *to hear*. See No. 4, 17, for the force of the first character.

38   In the TWO HANDS ; represented pictorially.

39   Of the GODDESSES ; as No. 29, 27, but in the plural, and without the D.S.

40   The TAIL ; S,T ; CHT, *a tail* ; preceded by the indefinite article, and followed by the D.S.

41   OF ; as No. 31, 9, &c.

42   The ASP ; as No. 31, 34.

43   THE SAME ; as 31, 35, but with a different T.

44   TWISTED ; EM, N,N ; perhaps from ⲖⲖOⲚⲖⲖEⲚ, anything *twisted* ; and followed by the D.S. of the asp's tail.

45   On the SCEPTRE ; as No. 31, 28.

Line 32.

1   THAT ; the pronoun following its substantive ; as No. 31, 11, &c.

2   BY WHICH ; as No. 30, 31, and 32.

3   ARRANGEMENT, in the plural, which is marked by S,M, in place of the more usual S,N. See No. 18, 12, where we have the same plural termination. But it is very possible that the M may be part of the following preposition in which case the final N is here wanting, or the M may be said to supply the sound wanted for both words at the same time ; as they were written by the ear, and not spelt grammatically. See No. 83, 7, and 8, for the similar beginning of a sentence.

4   IN ; N, as No. 28, 25 ; unless it be M,N, as at No. 7, 28. Here it forms a compound preposition, with the next word.

5   WITHIN ; S,H,N ; CAⲂOYⲚ. This and the former word together make one compound preposition, meaning *Between* ; and they may be compared to No. 7, 28, a similar compound preposition. The flower is an O at No. 2, 22, and is so placed that it might be taken for the vowel in this word. But it is necessary to take it as the substantive following it.

6   The EARS OF CORN ; as No. 31, 24, but the D.S. only, without the spelt word. Here the Greek has *The crown* ; but the two have the same meaning, as the ears of corn were to be placed upon the statue as its crown.

7   THAT, or rather THOSE, as its noun is in the plural.   See
No. 32, 1.   This pronoun following its substantive proves that
the flower is a word by itself, as described, and not the letter O,
part of the foregoing preposition, No. 32, 5.

8   May be SHOWN.   On the Rosetta Stone we have these three
characters in one, with the same meaning.   The sitting man holds
out the tablet with his outstretched arm.   In that case the character
is strictly pictorial.   Here it is less so.

9   THE; as No. 31, 7, &c.

10   NAME; being the oval within which the queen's name is
written; as No. 28, 18, &c.

11   OF; as No. 30, 23, &c.

12   BERENICE; as No. 31, 20, &c.

13   THE; as No. 32, 9, &c.

14   CHARACTERS, or CONSPICUOUS MARKS, written, as it would seem,
pictorially, by means of a peculiar character, then the plural sign,
and then the word *Conspicuous*.   The letter T may be the feminine
article.

15   OF; as No. 30, 2, &c.

16   The SCRIBES; as No. 18, 22, though at No. 37, 10, it means
letters.

17   OF, as No. 18, 23, &c.

18   HEAVENLY LIFE; as No. 18, 24.

═

19   AND.   In some cases it seems doubtful whether these letters,
A,O, are the article or the conjunction; but here it seems clear,
as at No. 2, 3.

20   DURING THE CELEBRATION.   The letters here are in an irregular
order; but on comparison with the Greek, we cannot be wrong in
recognizing I,O,T, *to keep* or *celebrate*, as No. 17, 21, and 32, 35,
&c.; and then the R,R, may be ЄƧΡΗΙ, *upon*, as No. 15, 10, &c.

21   Of the DAYS; as No. 22, 10, but in the plural.

22, 23.   The ceremony called in the Greek THE KIKELLIA, possibly
the festival already described in Lines 51 and 52 of the Greek, as
the same month is the time for each.   The first letters are K,A,
which correspond with the word *Kikellia*.

24   IN ; as No. 28, 15, &c.

25   The month of CHŒAC ; as No. 26, 2.

26   IN ADDITION TO ; as No. 15, 3, and 28, 44.

27   The WATER PROCESSION ; as No. 28, 29.

28   Of OSIRIS ; as No. 25, 5.

29   It shall be GRANTED ; as No. 9, 20. This must be distinguished
from No. 29, 43, where the hand does not hold the pyramid.

30   UNTO ; A,N ; the preposition $\overline{N}$, which is more usually, in
this inscription, written without the vowel, as No. 31, 29, &c.

31   The WOMEN ; as No. 31, 3.

32   The WIVES, as No. 4, 35. The Greek here has παρθενοι, a word
which in the Hellenistic dialect of Alexandria, was not limited to
unmarried maidens, but meant young women.

33   OF, as No. 32, 17, &c.

34   The PRIESTS ; as No. 30, 8, &c.

35   To PREPARE ; as No. 17, 21, and 32, 20, where we translate it,
to celebrate.

36   ANOTHER ; K,T,T ; KЄT, as No. 16, 27, &c. The second T may
be the feminine article, showing that the first T is part of the word.

37   STATUE ; as No. 31, 16.

38   OF ; as No. 31, 41, &c.

39   BERENICE ; as No. 31, 20, &c.

40   CHIEF ; E,T ; perhaps ЄЄT, may mean *Great*, though it is used
for *Pregnant*. Our hieroglyphical word is often met with, and
always with this meaning. Voc. 1372.

41   Of WOMEN ; as No. 32, 31.

42   PERFORMING, CELEBRATING ; as No. 32, 35, with S,N, for the
plural.

43   SACRIFICES ; as No. 26, 10.

44   AND ; as No. 30, 25, &c.

45   OTHER things ; as No. 20, 20, &c.

Line 33.

1   SHALL BE CELEBRATED ; as No. 28, 45, which has the prefix of
the infinitive mood, while here we have S, the prefix of the future
tense. No. 20, 22, is in the same tense.

2   UPON ; N,I,M ; ΠЄΜ ; as No. 2, 10, and 23, 11.

3   The DAYS; as No. 32, 21.

4   OF; as No. 32, 33, &c.

5   ASSEMBLY; as No. 28, 27, &c.

6   THAT; as No. 32, 1, &c.

═

7   BECAUSE OF THIS, BY THIS; as No. 32, 2, &c.

8   It is DECREED; as No. 32, 3; and as 9, 14, but we have another letter in addition.

9   BEHOLD; as No. 19, 8, &c.

10   FOR; E,M, instead of M, the more usual preposition, as No. 29, 38, &c.

11   OTHER; as No. 20, 20, but preceded by a K, which may be for KET, *other*, and thus give to the word a reduplicate form.

12   WOMEN; as No. 32, 31, &c.

13   Who ARE WILLING; EI, R,M; probably EI, *to be*, and ⲡⲁⲛ, *willing*. The M may be for N, as is not unusual.

14   Shall CELEBRATE; as No. 33, 1.

15   THEIR OWN; N,OU,OU; ⲛⲟⲩⲟⲩ; as No. 11, 1.

16   UNTO; as No. 29, 1, &c.

17   GODDESS; as No. 29, 27.

18   THAT SAME; the adjective to the foregoing substantive; as No. 29, 28, &c.

19   HYMNS; M, perhaps for ⲉⲙⲓ, *to remember*, preceded by R, the verb of action, and followed by S,N, for the plural. See No. 3,
.   19, and 28, 43, for this word *to celebrate*.

20   SING. The man in the act of praying is followed by the letters O,T, which must make some such word as ⲟⲩⲡⲟⲧ, *to sing*. See No. 34, 8, where this is confirmed.

21   To the GODDESS; as No. 33, 17.

22   THAT SAME; as No. 33, 18.

23   BEHOLD; as No. 33, 9.

24   UNDER; the preposition as No. 32, 30; which in other places is written without the vowel.

25   The PRIESTESSES. This is the word SET, No. 1, 12, in the feminine and with the D.S. They are therefore priestesses of the very first rank, as we shall be told at No. 33, 43.

26   CHOSEN ; as No. 30, 9.

27   Another class of PRIESTS, or, according to the Greek, *Priestesses;* possibly *Servants of the gods,* may be the literal rendering. The first letter is perhaps a B, and may represent ꞴⲰⲔ, *a servant.* As the hatchet, *God,* is pronounced NOU, the whole word may be *Bockanou,* the name of one of the four orders of priests, and written at length in Egypt. Inscript. pl. 32.   Here these servants are women.

28   Who CARRY ; as No. 30, 24, &c.

29   The prefix of the case, which, when the case is the accusative, we do not express in English ; but we treat it as a preposition when it represents any other case.

30   The THINGS THAT ARE CARRIED ; as No. 33, 28 ; in the Greek, *the necessaries.*

31   OF; as No. 33, 4, &c.

32   The GODS; as No. 30, 14, &c.

33   To whom THEY ARE APPOINTED; or DECREED; as No. 32, 3, &c.

34   FOR; as No. 33, 29, &c.

35   The PRIESTLY WOMEN; being the word *Priest,* as No. 30, 8, followed by the D.S. of a woman, and a double plural termination,
=

36   Is MADE; A,R, ⲈⲢⲈ; being the auxiliary prefix to the verb No. 33, 39, from which it is separated by the interjection and the nominative. See No. 25, 29, and 22, 6, in both which cases it is separated from its chief word.

37   BEHOLD; as No. 33, 9.

38   THE EARLY CORN, *the unripe seed,* is required by the Greek.

39   SPRUNG UP; R,T,E; ⲢⲎⲦ. This is the literal meaning of the word which we have so often rendered as *Added;* No. 32. 26, &c.

40   MADE itself CONSPICUOUS; the sitting figure *Conspicuous,* as No. 31, 22, &c. preceded by R,R,R, of which R may be the auxiliary verb *to make,* and R,R, the preposition ⲈⳘⲢⲎⲒ, as No. 15, 10, &c.

41   EARS OF CORN ; as No. 31, 24, but with a different D.S.

42   Shall BRING; A,N; ⲈⲒⲚⲈ, to *bring*. See No. 26, 32.

43   The PRIESTESSES; as No. 33, 25.

44   OF THE FIRST RANK; as No. 28, 35, &c., preceded by the indefinite article.

Line 34.

1   GIVE; as No. 32, 29, where it was preceded by the auxiliary verb.

2   UNTO; as No. 32, 11, &c.

3   The STATUE; as No. 31, 10, but without the D.S., which becomes less necessary when the word has been already written.

4   OF; as No. 31, 29, &c.

5   GODDESS; as No, 33, 17.

6   THE SAME; as No. 33, 18, &c.

7   SONGS; H,O,S; ϨⲰⲤ; and again at No. 34, 36.

8   SING; as No. 33, 20, though there the man is using his hands or praying, and here he points to his mouth. This figure is ⲢⲞ, *a mouth*, and with the O,T, which follow, and the addition of an article at the beginning, becomes ⲞⲨⲢⲞⲦ, *to sing*. The article ⲞⲨ was probably often in this way sounded when not written; as we have numerous instances in kings' names of the letters RA, the *sun*, being pronounced Phra, by the addition of the definite article

9   UNTO; as No. 34, 2, &c.

10   HER; P,E; ⲠⲈ, which in Coptic is masculine, *He, Him*. See No. 30, 17, where this word is also in the objective case.

11   The D.S., a sitting figure, without the head-dress distinctive of a woman, but made feminine by the S which follows it.

12   UPON, AT; as No. 32, 30.

13   APPOINTED; T,O,S, ⲦⲰϢ. For the force of the S, see No. 11, 40.

14   TIMES; probably the same character as the first in the word No. 29, 8, to which we have so often given that meaning.

15   These SONGS; as No. 34, 7.

16   The MEN and WOMEN shall SING; the man alone points to his mouth; but that may be enough to show that the women also are to sing.

17   The MEN; P,E; ⲠⲎ, *He*, in the plural, because of the three

dots. See No. 2, 7, for the force of the first letter, and No. 2, 10, for the force of the second.

18   The WIVES ; as No. 32, 32, &c.

19   In PLACES ; M,A, ꙇꙇꙋ, *a place.* The conjunction which follows, and separates this word from a similar word, namely, *assemblies,* proves its meaning. See No. 35, 4.

20   AND ; as No. 20, 19, &c.

21   ASSEMBLIES ; as No. 22, 25, &c.

22   CARRYINGS OUT ; as No. 33, 30, &c.

23   OF ; as No. 33, 31.

24   The GODS ; as No. 33, 32.

25   SONGS, or WORDS ; M,S ; with D.S. of a man in the act of prayer ; perhaps the S may be ϣⲱ to speak, with M, the prefix of the case.

26   FROM AMONG, or FROM THE BOTTOM. See No. 17, 17, where it is rendered *At first.* It is the preposition, or adverb, ⲥⲁⳉⲡ̄ⲏⲓ, and partakes of its very various meanings. The R,R is for II,R, as at No. 20, 24, &c.

27   WHICH ; N,T,T,E ; ⲛⲉⲧ ; the pronoun to the foregoing word *Songs.*

28   A MAN ; represented pictorially.

29   OF ; as No. 34, 23, &c.

30   HEAVENLY LIFE ; as No. 32, 18, &c.

31   Shall GIVE ; as No. 34, 1, &c.

32   UNTO ; as No. 34, 2, &c.

33   The CHIEF ; M,R ; ꙇⲁⲡⲉ ; as No. 2, 17, where it is preceded by the indefinite article. In other and earlier inscriptions these two letters are sometimes followed by a K ; and then the word resembles the Hebrew מלך. See Voc. 680.

34   LEARNED MAN ; S,B,E ; ⲥⲃⲱ·

85   OF ; as No. 34, 23, &c.

36   The SINGERS ; as No. 34, 15, and 16.

37   To WRITE ; see *Scribe,* No. 36, 29.

38   A COPY ; H,T,T ; from ⳉⲉ, *like,* as No. 15, 4. See No. 31, 36.

39   THE ; as No. 31, 7, &c.

40   BOOKS ; as No. 37, 12. Voc. 335.

I

41   OF; as No. 34, 29, &c.

42   HEAVENLY LIFE; as No. 34, 30.

=

43   BECAUSE OF THIS; as No. 33, 7, &c.

44   When are DISTRIBUTED; A,T,O,T; perhaps from ⲦⲞⲓ, *to distribute*, with E, the prefix of the verb's mood; or perhaps ⲧϩⲓⲱⲧ *to place*, a verb formed of ⲦⲎⲓ, *to give*, and ϩⲓⲱⲧ, *upon.*

45   DEDICATED LOAVES. The first character, O, is a very frequent abridgment of ⲞⲨⲞⲦⲉⲃ, No. 25, 1; the second is a loaf represented pictorially, as No. 35, 38.

46   UNTO; as No. 34, 9, &c.

47   The PRIESTS; as No. 32, 34, &c.

48   FROM; as No. 33, 34, &c.

49   THE; as No. 28, 8, &c.

50   TEMPLES; as No. 29, 4, &c.

51   Of the FAMILY; as No. 26, 20.

52   Those ALREADY; as No. 14, 8; and 16, 21, where it is in the singular, and as No. 14, 20, when it is in the plural, as here.

Line 35.

1   OF; the preposition ⲛ, as No. 32, 30; or it may be ⲉⲓⲛⲉ, *Is brought*, as No. 33, 42.

2   The SET, or CHIEF PRIEST, as No. 8, 24; and distinguished as there by his peculiar crown. But here the Greek has "When they are brought out to the multitude." The scribe seems to have been confused between this word for *Priest*, and ⲱⲱ, *a multitude.* The two meanings, which the last word will bear, leave us in the difficulty.

3   Of the TEMPLE; as No. 25, 38; but here preceded by the article.

4   Of a PLACE; E,M,I, or M,E,I; for the vowel, written across the M may be read in either place; ⲙⲁⲓ, *a place*, preceded by the article. See No. 34, 19.

5   There shall be DISTRIBUTED; as No. 34, 44.

6   PRESENCE; N,R; ⲛⲁϩⲣⲉ, a preposition composed of ⲛⲁ, *belonging* to, and ϩⲣⲁ, *the face.* It is used as the adjective to the following word *Loaves*; and it thus describes them as brought

into the temple into the presence of the statue. It is the counter-part of the Hebrew לפני, *unto the face*, from which the bread of the temple was called לחם פנים, *presence-bread*. See No. 35, 23; but see also No. 14, 35, where these letters are a verbal prefix. The doubt between the two meanings is removed by the D.S.

7   LOAVES; represented pictorially, as at No. 36, 10, where this character is used as the D.S. after the word spelt by letters.

8   UNTO; as No. 34, 32, &c.

9   The DAUGHTERS; M,S,O, plural; from ꞩꞧEC, *born*. See No. 13, 29, *Birth*, also No. 37, 44, *Children*. The O is the plural termination, and is very unnecessarily followed by the three dots.

10   Of the CHIEFS; as No. 32, 40. This is usually, perhaps always, a feminine title.

11   OF; as No. 34, 23, &c.

12   The PRIESTS; as No. 34, 47, &c.

13   SINCE; as No. 24, 16, and 14, 25.

14   The DAY; as No. 33, 3, &c.

15   When THEY WERE BORN; as No. 35, 9.

16   WAS REMEMBERED, or CELEBRATED; as No. 29, 19. Thus it would seem that their right to food was not counted from their birthday, but from some ceremonial festival which soon followed it, like the day of baptism among Christians.

17   FROM; as No. 34, 48, &c.

18   THE; as No. 34, 49, &c.

19   SACRED DEDICATED LOAVES; being composed of the words *God*, No. 33, 32; and *Dedicated loaves*, No. 34, 45. In the copy of the Decree at Paris, we find here, instead of the two words, *Dedicated Loaves*, the word No. 14, 34, in the plural, *Appointed things*.

20   OF; as No. 35, 11, &c.

21   The GODS; as No. 33, 32, &c. In the Paris copy this word is written with three hatchets, and without the three dots.

22   OUT OF; as No. 25, 44. In the Paris copy we have the owl instead of this character.

23   THE PRESENCE-LOAVES; as No. 35, 6, and 7. They are called in the Greek *the sacred revenue.*

24   Marked with a PATTERN. This meaning we learn from

No. 36, 6. The cross may be the D.S. of the pattern on each loaf or cake. The pricked cakes, so often mentioned in the Hebrew Law, as in Leviticus vii., 12, do not seem to have been marked with any pattern, but simply pricked, to make them less heavy, because they were not made with leaven. These Egyptian loaves may be compared rather to the Christian crossed-buns eaten on Good Friday.

25   ADJUDGED; as No. 16, 47, and 22, 16.

26   BY; as No. 32, 30.

27   The PRIESTS; as No. 35, 12, &c.

28   The SENATORS; as No. 16, 2.

29   IN; as No. 30, 21, &c.

30   The SANCTUARY, or cell of the temple; as No. 28, 31, and 16, 32.

31   Of the TWO REGIONS, of Upper and Lower Egypt; being the word *Land*, followed by the dual sign.

32   UPON; as No, 29, 7, &c.

33   The TIMES; as No. 29, 8; meaning, as it would seem, *henceforth.*

34   LIKE or AGREEABLY TO; as No. 31, 36, and 27, 6.

35   The MOUTH, meaning the COMMAND; R,E; ρο, the *mouth.*

36   OF; as No. 34, 32, &c.

37   The PRIESTS of the DEDICATED LOAVES; though there is nothing to distinguish this word from No. 35, 19, where the loaves were meant. In the Greek we have *Priests of the revenue.*

38   The LOAVES; A,K; ΔΙΚ, *bread,* followed by the D.S. and the three dots. Without the D.S. it could not be distinguished from the word *Dedication.*

39   Which ARE GIVEN; as No. 9, 20; but distinct from No. 29, 43.

Line 36.

1   UNTO; as No. 35, 36, &c.

2   The WIVES; as No. 34, 18, with the addition of the D.S.

3   OF; as No. 35, 11, &c.

4   The PRIESTS; as No. 35, 27, &c.

5   Shall be MARKED; as No. 28, 24, &c., as it would seem, though the order of the last two letters is reversed. There and elsewhere it is rendered *to celebrate,* as of a festival.

6 With a PATTERN; according to the Greek. See No. 35, 24, and 22, 15, where the Greek does not help us.

7 To be IMPRESSED; M,K,F; perhaps from KⲰ, *to put on*, preceded by M, the sign of the infinitive mood, and followed by F, for the third person singular. See No. 36, 13, for a word of the same grammatical form.

8 UPON the LOAF; *Upon*, as No. 36, 1, &c.; *Loaf*, as No. 35, 38.

9 PUT THEREON; as No. 30, 39, where we have remarked that this word is often of no use but to add emphasis.

10 The LOAVES; as No. 35, 38, where the letters have the same force, though different in form.

11 OF; as No. 30, 40, &c.

12 BERENICE; as No. 32, 39, &c.

13 To BE NAMED; see No. 23, 44. This is a word of the same form as No. 36, 7, beginning with the sign of the infinitive, and ending with that of the third person singular.

—

14 The LEARNED PROPHET; S,B,E,O; cⲂⲰ, *learned*, while the figure, pointing to his mouth, tells us that he is a speaker.

15 THAT SAME; as No. 32, 1.

16 OF; as No. 30, 31, &c.

17 The PLACE; as No. 35, 4.

18 Another D.S. of this prophet.

19 The SCRIBE; as No. 32, 16, &c.

20 CONSECRATED; O,T,F; being the same as O,T,P, No. 25, 1. ⲰⲦⲂ, *to dedicate*. This is very possibly the original, though less usual, way of writing the word; as it may be a past participle of OⲨOⲦ, *to separate*.

21 Of the SENATORS; as No. 35, 28.

22 OF; as No. 25, 44, &c., meaning the *representatives of*, as we see there had been only twenty, and were for the future to be only twenty-five senators to represent the whole priesthood of the kingdom.

23 The PRIESTS OF THE TEMPLES. The character for temples is here used as an adjective descriptive of the man that follows.

24 ALL; as No. 18, 8.

25   The CHIEF; as No. 34, 33.

26   Of the TEMPLE-YARD; as No. 29, 4, &c. But here used in opposition to No. 36, 23, and therefore the general word *Temple* is unsuitable. It is an adjective to the figure of a man that follows, as No. 36, 23.

27   The PRIESTS; being the figure of a man distinguished by the foregoing adjective. The distinction between the Temples of No. 36, 23, and those of No. 36, 26, is not explained. We can observe however, that the first represents a standing building, and the other only a ground plan, perhaps a court-yard, as distinguished from the building that stood within it. In this way the upper and lower ranks of priests seem to be distinguished.

28   AND; as No. 34, 20, &c.

29   The SCRIBES; as No. 32, 16; but here followed by the D.S. of a man.

30   OF; as No. 36, 3, &c.

31   The TEMPLES; here described as *sacred buildings;* as No. 35, 3. In the copy of the Decree at Paris this word is slightly enlarged, being written as No. 26, 23.

32   Shall CARVE; O, CH,T; followed by the D.S. of a chisel and a slab of stone; from ЄКШT *a builder.* See No. 12, 32, *Lord of the builders.*

33   THE; as No. 31, 7, &c.

34   INSCRIPTION; SH, A,A,T; from CⳔHT, *a writing.* See No. 21, 23, for the force of the first letter.

Line 37.

1   On a TABLET; represented pictorially, as on the Rosetta Stone.

2   OF; as No. 34, 4, &c.

3   STONE; A,N,R; with D.S.; ШNI, *stone.* The force of the R is not evident; it might possibly make the word into *Hewn stone* from IPI *to make.*

5   COPPER; but how to be read is uncertain; R,E,P,O,E, plural. The latter letters may perhaps represent ⳒⲀЄOOⲨ, *bright;* and the plural sign has the force of OU.

6   IN; as No. 34, 48, &c.

7   LETTERS; as No. 36, 29, where it is part of the word *Scribe.*

8   OF; as No. 36, 30, &c.

9   HEAVENLY LIFE; as No. 34, 30, &c. These "letters of heavenly life " are the Hieroglyphics.

10 LETTERS; as No. 37, 7, &c.

11 FOR; as No. 35, 36, &c.

12 BOOKS; as No. 34, 40. These "letters for books " are the enchorial, or common running hand, seen upon the papyrus-rolls. This portion of the inscription was never executed on this tablet, which has only two out of the three portions. On the tablet at Paris all three inscriptions were duly carved.

13 LETTERS; as No. 37, 10.

14 FOR; as No. 37, 11, &c.

15 The GREEKS; or possibly for Lower Egypt; as that plant is sometimes typical of that district.

16 The auxiliary verb to the coming word, from ΘΡΕ, *to make* ; as No. 29, 43. The letters are not in the order of the Coptic word. This must be distinguished from No. 35, 39, where the hand holds a pyramid.

17 To be SET UP, as in the Rosetta Stone. See also No. 29, 24, for the first character.

18 In a CONSPICUOUS; according to the Greek, which fixes the meaning of this character for the other parts of this inscription.

19 PLACE; the M used for the longer word of No. 35, 4, and 36, 17 ; and followed by a D.S.

20 OF; as No. 36, 30, &c.

21 MEN and WOMEN; as No. 22, 43, &c.

22 IN; as No. 37, 6, &c.

23 The TEMPLES; as No. 34, 50. This, we see, is the word in its widest sense, including temples of the very various kinds distinguished by the other names herein used.

24 Of the FIRST RANK; as No. 25, 13.

25 TEMPLES; as No. 37, 23, and No. 28, 34, the change in the letter M making no difference in the word.

26 Of the SECOND RANK; distinguished by the dual sign.

27 TEMPLES; as No. 37, 23, &c.

28 Of the THIRD RANK; distinguished by the three dots.

29   So that there may be GIVEN; as No. 35, 39, but preceded by an R, which may be the preposition.

30   Perhaps, a SIGHT, if we may consider the eye as the D.S. of the foregoing word.

31   THE; as No. 36, 33; perhaps *Of it.*

32   ALL; N,E,B; ꟿꟷ; as No. 30, 34.

33   MEN and WOMEN; as No. 30, 35, and followed by the word *All*, in a shorter form than No. 30, 36.

34   How TO PREPARE; as No. 5, 11, &c., and preceded by M, the sign of the infinitive mood.

35   BY; as we must make the sentence conform to the Greek; but it would seem, from the order of the words, more like *For.*

36   The PRIESTS; as No. 30, 8, &c.

37   OF; as No. 36, 30, &c.

38   The TEMPLES; as No. 37, 23, &c.

39   Of the CITIES; as No. 5, 33,

40   Of EGYPT; as No. 5, 34.

41   FOR; as No. 31, 29, &c.

42   The GODS EUERGETÆ; as No. 1, 31, &c.

43   AND; as No. 36, 28, &c.

44   Their CHILDREN, both male and female, as shown by the D.S. From M,S, *born;* see No. 35, 9, &c.

45   BEHOLD; as No. 33, 9, &c.; but with a different A.

46   The RELIGIOUS CEREMONIES; as No. 19, 1, and 28, 45.

47   FOR; as No. 37, 14, &c.

48   The DOINGS; as No. 4, 38, and 17, 33.

Woodfall and Kinder, Printers, Milford Lane, Strand, London, W.C